Signs Unseen, Sounds Unheard

By Carolyn Brimley Norris

Second Printing, 1985

ISBN 0-933076-02-9

Library of Congress Number 81-65544

The author welcomes your comments.
Write care of Alinda Press.

Printed in the United States of America

This book is dedicated to

Gerilee Gustason,
who listens with her heart,

Esther Zawolkow,
who was almost born signing,

and
Frank Caccamise, adviser and friend

Carolyn Brimley Norris, Ph.D. lives in northern California with her botanist husband and two large dogs. She illustrates, edits, and publishes materials concerning sign-language communication. She taught literature and writing at Gallaudet College for the deaf during a decade of college and university teaching. Her father's late deafness led her to Gallaudet, and this is her second novel drawn from consultations with deaf people, following *Island of Silence*, 1976. She will have three other novels published in 1980-81. Both Norrises are involved in marathon running.

Sketches are self-portraits of deaf children ages five to ten.
Poetry by deaf adults.

Acknowledgements

This book was developed during 5 years through the guidance, example, and editing of many people. Only a few can be thanked here.

Deaf adults: Carolyn Hunter, Nancy Kelly-Jones, Bill White, Bunny White, Jane Locke, Lawrence Newman, Paddy Ladd, King Jordan, Dolly Mason, Kathy Barrett, the Glovers, Bert Neathery, Dennis Waterhouse.

Deaf children: Lynn Spradley, Bobi Pfetzing, Brandy Olson, Jesse Thomas, Jenny Reynolds, Debby Garcia.

Parents of deaf children and children of deaf parents: Tom and Louise Spradley, Joyce Groode, Carol Ferreir, Louie Fant, Carl Kirchner, Mary Anne Locke, Raili Ojala, Ruth Schieberl, the Reynolds, Roberta Thomas, Rhonda Bennett, Don Olson, Ruth Saunders, Jackie Mendelsohn.

and teachers, writers, and editors: Kay Meadow, Herbert Kohl, Irene Goodman, Robert Fintzy, Anna Hansen, Mary Alward, Signe Birch, Pirjo Nuotio, Martin Colville, Nicholas Callow, and Merl Keller, plus the Northcoast Writers who listened to so many drafts read.

The staff and children at the following schools taught me a great deal: the Danish Center for Total Kommunication and Kosterskole (Copenhagen), Kuulonhuoltoliitto (Helsinki), the Jack Ashley School (London), and the Victorian School for Deaf Children (Melbourne). In the U.S., WPSD, CSD at Riverside, San Rafael, Ridgewood, Kendall and Taft Schools were particularly enlightening. Enthusiastic friends at Eureka Printing Company deserve a thanks as well.

Heard melodies are sweet, but those unheard
  Are sweeter; therefore, ye soft pipes, play on;
Not to the sensual ear, but, more endeared,
  Pipe to the spirit ditties of no tone:
Fair youth, beneath the trees, thou canst not leave
  Thy song, nor ever can those trees be bare;
  Bold lover, never, never canst thou kiss,
Though winning near the goal—yet, do not grieve;
  She cannot fade, though thou hast not thy bliss,
For ever wilt thou love, and she be fair!

from John Keats, “Ode on a Grecian Urn,” 1819

One solitary road to go alone,
lost within a sea of silent moving words,
facial hieroglyphs.

Mervin D. Garretson

Nicky

Nicky Strathgordon ran through chilly, wet, green-smelling grass that was too dark to see. He couldn't see anything except that no one was chasing him yet. He ran fast, afraid he'd see lights flash on suddenly in the house, a blacker blob in the black night behind him. Desperately he ran.

Looking back and looking back, he remembered dogs. Dogs could strike him before he knew it, so he walked on the road as soon as he found the road. He found it by stumbling over the edge and falling flat. Because his hands were stuck out in front of him, his face didn't quite hit the ground, but when he got up, his knees and wrists stung, and he had to feel where the road really started.

He followed the edge in the dark as if he were a blind kid.

When the first car-lights came, Nicky jumped sideways, his throat choking for fear they'd capture him, but the car kept right on going. He didn't want anybody to stop. Even a good person would lean over and flutter-fluttering ask him why he was out so late at night, all alone.

The driver would ask, "How old are you?" like always, and if he said, "Nine, almost ten," so anyone understood, they'd think he lied, because he was little. People all thought he was seven, not nine.

Breezes lifted Nicky's hair off his forehead as he ran, but sweat stuck his hair down. When he stopped to rest, he shivered; his palms got all wet inside his fists.

He figured the lump he left in his bed would look like him. Daddy came sometimes, making the hall light flash in his face, then standing there and looking at him. He could have fooled Daddy if he'd put pillows in his bed, but he put his plastic astronaut there instead. It was better. Almost as big as him.

Mama said always walk facing traffic, so he did, running only when his side stopped hurting. He jumped behind bushes to hide from cars, but the bushes and weeds were awful wet. He kept looking behind for somebody chasing.

It was exciting being up so late and outdoors alone, if you weren't scared. The moon was playing tag up there with the clouds, and no rain was lucky. He told himself that, over and over, while cars and trucks blew him sideways and said "Hmmmm" in his head. Their lights showed the road ahead of him, which was round in the middle and so shiny it was like walking down the back of a big, black snake.

He'd been smart to get out of that window. It was on the first floor, but high above the ground. He'd pulled the screen off from inside, yesterday, and hid it under his bed. Then he got the little ladder from the broom-closet and put that in his room. Leaning out the window tonight, he had lowered the little ladder, on a rope he got from Daddy's workshop. Then he hung himself out the window, holding with his elbows and reaching toes down to the ladder. Thinking about that made him less scared. He sure could take care of himself.

Pretty soon Nicky began to rub his eyes, tired of the million white bright lights coming at him, making him scrunch down in wet-grass. After an hour or two or three, the cars got fewer, so he walked on the road, out of the wet. He got cold, and his feet slipped round all squishy in his shoes; he wished he'd brought a jacket and dry socks.

He kept following the glow in the sky that his sister Elyse said means a city is underneath. Knoxville at night wouldn't be safe. He'd try to ride a bus home. To Pittsburgh. But bus-stations are never good places for a kid alone. "Don't stare at strangers. Don't take candy from anyone. Don't get in a car with a stranger," he'd been told all his life, but everyone in Knoxville would be a stranger, and if he didn't want cops chasing him, he'd have to play-act.

Pretend he was not handicapped, that he was what people called "normal." He wanted his ear-level aids, to let him hear trucks and thunder, but his brown hair wasn't grown long enough yet to cover them, so he'd left them behind.

Nicky felt like crying. He'd been here ages and ages without talking with Daddy. Grandpa Katz said Daddy could learn from Nicky, now, even better than from a teacher, but he'd found out Grandpa was wrong.

It's bad to hate your real Daddy, but Nicky was afraid he did.

What was really scary was when Daddy took away his pad and pencil and held him by the chin so it pinched, and made funny mouths when he talked. Then the strange man came. Nicky couldn't figure him out. He talked, but his eyes went round and round like a deaf person's. He didn't move his hands, and when Nicky signed to him, he slapped down his hands so hard Nicky cried.

He'd searched for a pencil, or any pen or crayon in the house. You can write on anything, on napkins and magazines and walls, but not without a pencil. Instead, he tried tomato juice on the dining-room wall, but that was too thin and didn't show, so next he used chocolate syrup. Daddy spanked him for that. Hard.

By then Nicky knew he didn't have a mother anymore, and step-father would turn out bad. Grandma and Grandpa gave him up real easy, and now Daddy hated him.

He didn't see anything coming.

That was when the thing hit him.

His heart jumped into his throat, tasting like blood. When teeth grabbed his leg, he jumped, yelled, and started running. It hit him again with teeth, and his sleeve tore. Fur brushed his arm and his face when he fell down and kicked at legs, screaming too hard to breathe. Then the dog or something wasn't there in the dark any longer. Maybe it was a lion or tiger come out of the trees. He scrambled up and ran faster, his sleeve flapping on his arm. Running made him warm again, so he stopped shaking.

When the sun began to come up, he was glad; you can't see dogs with the moon gone to bed. He could tell east and west, now, but which way was Knoxville? No one was awake to help him. People pull away and frown and shake heads, and don't understand; they might call him M.R., slow in the mental. If he asked for paper to write a note, people would see he wasn't mental, but deaf, then hearies make wide mouths like for "Yum yum," and smack-smack lips. That kills any chance of reading them. He'd have to pretend to be a hearie.

He must also search for a deaf person or smart hearie, now he was seeing some gas stations and churches. He still had to watch for horrible dogs to come out and tell everyone in bark-talk that he was a stranger, flap-flapping mouths; he must look at tails and hair on backs to know if they barked friendly or barked mean. He wanted to run from them, but they'd chase, because they can smell fear. He tried to smell very brave.

His road suddenly met a big, wide highway, and a bus passed with a swoosh of air; it said "Knoxville." It was going the opposite direction from the way Nicky had turned, so he spun around and went the same direction as the bus, wrinkling his nose at its gas-fart.

Near the top of one hill, he watched a man's head grow right up out of the highway like a flower, and then his body came up, and then a motorcycle. Nicky always liked to watch that happen, but today he was tired and starving and didn't even smile.

He dreamed of seeing deaf people with words like pictures flowing off their fingers. Even one deaf person walking all alone looks different from any hearie. More "observant," Leah spelled it. Hearies just scratched, or held cigarettes, or wiped noses.

Then Nicky found a bus station. It wasn't for the dog-bus he came on, but was named "Trailways." He stood still and planned. He'd have to use the ten-dollar bill he got from Daddy's wallet to buy a ticket home. Before he went in, he practiced the word he'd have to say. Just one word.

For "P," you press lips together without sound and puff out air with a pop. Then you turn on the little motor in your throat, like teachers say, putting your hand on your neck to feel it going. That makes sound, like a cat's purr. Next sound is not closed like "oo" or open like "ahh," but in between. Let that out for a little while, and try to do "T," with your tongue stopping the air. Push more sound out over tongue-tip, wetly, supposed to be "S." Then comes another lips-together with sound, popping open, and then the "G" in the throat that no one can see, but it flips like a burp.

He forgot the "R," but "R" is the hardest letter to say, when you've never heard one.

"Pittsburgh."

(Mama once laughed, "Good thing that you don't come from 'Philadelphia'!") If only he dared to climb on a bus and scrunch down in back, without trying to communicate. He'd be happy to pay the whole ten dollars, but making people think he wasn't deaf would be the scariest thing he ever did.

A line of people were waiting for the counter-man. He stood in line to wait his turn, but when he got there the counter was so high Nicky didn't think his mouth would show over the edge. On tiptoes, he took out all his bills and put them up on the counter. He sucked in a big chestful of air and got ready to make his wonderful correct voice for "Pittsburgh."

He gave the kind-faced man behind the counter a brave look, and then he said the word.

The man gave a little jerk like someone hit him. Other people looked around, too. Even kids. So he'd made sound, all right, but all he wanted was this one man to give him one Pittsburgh ticket.

"Flutter-flutter" all the lips said, and the man leaned over the counter, staring at Nicky's bill. He might have said, "Where's your mother?" or "Where do you want to go?" It started with "Where," for sure. People came over closer and looked down at him.

He poked his money and said "Pittsburgh" again, but not so well. It didn't feel right in his mouth, like he'd practiced. He knew the second try wasn't even like "paper," which was how Elyse said that word sounded. He was afraid to use deaf-voice to say, "I want a ticket to Pittsburgh." His mouth got so dry it stuck shut.

It was like a shock of electricity when someone grabbed him from behind. He was lifted up so he could get his arms on the counter on each side of his money.

"PITTSBURGH!" he said again, straining, and then he gave up pretending hearie and made writing motions. The man had a pen in his pocket and lots of paper just out of Nicky's reach.

No one did anything. He pushed the money forward a little ways. The man shook his head no. No, something. What? Nicky craned around to see who held him; it was an old man in a grey suit. His mouth was going like mad, but all Nicky got was warm mouth-breath. Everyone moved hands, but not to show what they were saying, so excited. Nicky wanted to cry, but he sure wouldn't get a ticket being a crybaby.

Now the bus-man said, "How old are you?" so it showed very clearly, and Nicky answered, "Twelve."

He expected everyone to laugh and never believe him, but they didn't do anything except stare with big eyes.

Recovering his money, he kicked a little. Everyone shook heads, and someone smelled of strong perfume. His ribs hurt where the man held him up. Once he got his money back, the man let him slowly down. He didn't even look up at faces before he ran for the door. He ran between buses that all had their doors shut tight, and ran out into the alley.

And then he was alone to cry, so Nicky cried and ran at the same time.

Lanier

Lanier Strathgordon was awakened in the middle of the night by a barking dog. Out here beyond the suburbs, barking was one of the few sounds you could hear, day or night. The nearest county road lay well below the house, beyond their lush, sloping lawn, its sparse traffic muted by distance and trees. He listened intently.

Many dogs now barked frantically in serial fashion, making an almost pleasant concert of canine voices. Now four of them went at it. The first barking faded, the second kept up its cry, and now a third and fourth dog, farther away, added their woofing. The deep-voice must be "Sir," the German Shepherd.

Probably someone was out for a midnight walk, stirring them up. Or a bicycler was pedaling down the road. Dogs detest bicyclers, or late-night joggers, panting past.

The fourth dog became barely audible before a fifth joined in, maybe a mile away. "Nocturne in D Major for Five Dogs in the Night"?

His little son Nicky, at least, wouldn't have his sleep disturbed. Nicky had never heard a dog bark.

(That realization, like hundreds before, hit Lanier in the gut.) Nor ever heard a bird sing or a person speak. Difficult as it was to have Nicky with them, life was more meaningful, now. Annalee, his bride of less than a year, shared his task, and Lanier's admiration for his wife grew at the same rate that frustration with Nicky increased. Immediately after the ceremony, Annalee had begun talking about babies, but now she kept busy helping her step-son. Janie's child. Plump, placid, blonde Annalee even looked pretty, sitting holding Nicky, speaking very precisely to him and restraining those infuriating little hands. Madonna.

"I might as well not have poured out tens of thousands in alimony to keep Janie home with Nicky," he'd told Annalee. He had also remained single, the only way he could afford alimony. But in spite of his sacrifices, Nicky's education was a failure. Could he and Annalee, working together as a team, salvage anything for the child? Experts made it sound relatively easy. Relative to what? was the question. He knew one thing, at least, struggling together sure did good things for this marriage. Annalee was not Janie. She listened to reason and showed both common sense and patience.

Lanier very quietly slid from his bed, found his slippers by feel in the dark, so as not to wake Annalee, and crept from the room and down the carpeted stairs. Thick carpeting, midnight-green or whatever they called it. He loved deep carpets, loved the whole cozy house, its mellow lamplight and dark corners, its brick fireplace and dazzling clean bathrooms.

He smiled. For five years after the divorce he'd come home from work to furnished rooms carpeted in underwear, to solidifying coffee-grounds and rings around tubs. Quickly he learned how much effort goes into making houses comfortable. Making them homes. Living as a bachelor, a divorce-o—the male version of divorcee—he forgot to put things back in the refrigerator and turn off the electric blanket; he let himself run out of sugar, butter and eggs, though at SG Systems, Inc., he never let his inventory fall dangerously low.

He'd married Janie at twenty, between college degrees, and divorce, twenty-five years later, showed him how monogamous, domestic, and home-centered he was. Now he was building himself another nest. The minute Janie got engaged to some guy named Steve, he found himself a fiancee. Annalee, who clerked in his store. Annalee Kratt.

Wife? Check. House? His first two-story, with age on it, and character, and an acre of land around it. Child? None, so far, until Nicky came. Choirs of angels sang. Beautiful, tiny Nicky, with that Bobby-Kennedy fall of hair and spaniel eyes. Nicky looked like him at nine, but his hair was thinning now, and he wore glasses and let out his belts. Only Annalee judged him "handsome."

Janie left Nicky with her parents in Kentucky during her honeymoon cruise with Steve Bratt. Then Grandma—a mother-in-law he was not sorry to exchange for Annalee's sweet old Momsy—needed gall-bladder surgery. Day five of Nicky's stay in Lexington, and Dad's plea to keep his son during Janie's absence now was heard. They asked Nicky. Nicky wanted very much to come visit his "real Daddy," so, dressed in his best clothes, brushed, polished, tagged, and put on a plane, the boy came flying into Lanier's arms in Knoxville. He held Nicky for the first time in a year, weeping in full view of everyone. Annalee wept, too.

"I want to fight for custody. I want my son," Lanier said. "Now I'm married, I have a home for him." Annalee sniffled and nodded, and hugged Nicky, wincing only a little at gyrating hands accompanied by inexplicable sounds.

Nicky did not talk coherently. Not so anyone, including his father, could understand him. Nicky still was dependent on sign language. But that could be changed. It had to be.

Downstairs in the hallway, Lanier remembered that he didn't need to tiptoe any longer. Nicky couldn't hear him. Only light awoke the child, or thumps. Vibrations. Lanier sighed when he saw the chair tucked under the knob of the door to Nicky's bedroom, to keep it securely shut.

He removed the chair cautiously, turned off the hall light, came back, and opened the door. There was Nicky, a mound in the moonlight, sleeping very soundly by the open window. He resisted the urge to go to his son and smooth his hair, cluck over him like a hen or mother, and take him into his arms. Try to. Nicky didn't want that, lately. Not from Daddy, and seldom from Annalee, either. Daddy retreated. Two-ten a.m.

He replaced the chair against the door to prevent the child's rampaging through the house all night, awakening them, hunting for heaven's knows what, lost in a weird, silent world.

He was thirsty for a cup of orange-clove tea, made with a immersion teaspoon. He would take a cup of tea up to his wife, but she hadn't roused. She needed sleep, after long hours shut up at home with Nicky's temper-fits and tantrums. He left work early each day so he could be back before four and spend maximum time with Nicky, who resisted bedtimes, staying up til ten. Well, it was summer, no school.

Tonight Nicky had seemed surprisingly docile about going to bed. Last night, rather. He was tucked in by nine-forty, and his father and step-mother played a game of Scrabble before bed. Maybe this presaged a change for the better.

Sitting at the breakfast bar, chin between his hands, he calculated exactly where he now stood. Wife, Home, Child. A beautiful, willful, wordless child. Not silent, but able to produce only long strings of vowels: "Ahheeoooeeeahh." Janie's product. Say it. A deaf-mute. Deaf-and-dumb. Horrible labels, but true. People stared, pitying the Strathgordons.

What had Janie said when Nicky was three, at the end of their marriage?

"You aren't Nicky's father. His father is a twelve-year-old boy."

That floored him, until he realized she meant Kirby. Kirby, their first child. Kirby acted as Nicky's father, because, as Janie put it, "Kirby wants to communicate with Nicky."

And he himself didn't? "Wrong, Janie. Wrong, wrong, wrong. Wrong, Janie, whom I loved so much, and grew almost to hate, but whom I now understand."

Janie's German measles during pregnancy had done it, or her genes, the doctors thought. She didn't know about her real father's family. Bert Katz was her step-father, and Charlotte Katz didn't talk about her first husband who died young. Or who wasn't her husband. No matter. There had never appeared on the Strathgordon side anyone like Nicky. "Your wife is burdened with guilt for bearing an imperfect child," said their second marriage-counselor. "She can be expected to act irrationally."

How long can you live with an irrational wife who is ruining the life of your child?

Nicky's deafness was diagnosed early. Grandma Katz suspected, tests were run, and there it was. No hearing. Almost zero. Kirby was nine, Leah and Elyse seven and six. "He doesn't act like the other children," Grandma said. Nicky was unplanned. Now the older three were lost to him totally, immersed in rock music, motorcycling, TV shows, and probably drugs. Nicky was the only one still innocent, young enough to be helped, to need a Daddy.

In a sign-language class once, the only man there, he discovered he had twenty toes. Fingers adept with word-processors and computers were no more adept here than if they were toes. But there were lots of things Janie and the kids could do that he could not, like roller-skate, play the piano, and sing. Was inability grounds for eviction from his home and the loss of his wife and four kids?

Lanier took the tea pot off the burner before the whistle could be heard upstairs, poured water over the perforated spoon, and sat looking into the steaming cup, eyes blind. Too old, at forty-four, to want to have a child by Annalee, he faced many more years of child-support. Annalee, well past thirty, might have a complicated pregnancy or an imperfect baby. Another handicapped child, one with some visible, incurable handicap, not an invisible one, like deafness, that could be overcome.

Authorities said Nicky could become normal. Could pass for hearing.

For years, he'd lugged books home, like a schoolboy: "Look, Janie, see?" "There's a course for parents like us; here's a new book on lipreading, an ad for a better amplifier. Look, Janie, look. See, Janie, see. Oral schools make children oral."

His expensive hearing aids Nicky tore out of his ears and once even flushed down the toilet. Lanier wasn't sure if at Nicky's so-called school the children even wore their aids all day.

He saw Janie standing there with her beautiful face enraged, her sweet lips getting thinner and thinner, as she hissed, "He's learning! He's getting knowledge. Know-ledge! He's at the head of his preschool class! We're all so PROUD of Nicky!"

"But just listen to him!" he'd wail. "I can't understand my son speak!"

After the divorce, she got custody because he was ill with wretchedness; then Janie forbade him to take Nicky out of the Pittsburgh house until he could "communicate" with the boy. Seeing Nicky on Janie's turf proved a very unpleasant ordeal for them all.

Result? In six years he'd seen Nicky for maybe a total of ten days, say fifty hours. He wasn't sure Nicky understood one thing he said. He never understood more than a few sounds Nicky made. They did a lot of ball-tossing, back and forth, and hugging, and eating in each other's tense company, and Nicky smiled thank-you for gifts, but that was all.

Like a starving man tasting food he's not allowed to swallow.

He told Janie that, aloud, as if she were standing right there with him, in the blue and gold dressing-gown he'd given her to set off her tennis-tan. "To see a child of mine and not know him at all is worse than if he'd died!"

That had been a wrong thing to say. Janie had thrown a fit, and the kids covered their ears. Kirby, with a black look, turned down Nicky's chest-amplifer, as if Nicky with or without amplification could hear a freight-train at full throttle rip through the house.

Lanier climbed slowly back up stairs, running his hand along the bannister—wide, golden maple. He'd lifted Nicky onto this bannister and helped the boy for the first time slide down. The delighted little face seemed to indicate that this was new to Nicky. It did the bannister no damage. Nicky learned quickly, and galloped upstairs again and again to slide down the bannister by himself. Again and again.

The wall facing the bannister had not fared as well. Lanier traced with a fingertip the faint chocolate stains that Annalee labored over for hours, using every scouring powder advertised on the tube. Under the colorful, framed Strathgordon coat of arms Nicky had written, "I hate you. Take me home." Written, not said.

He managed to get back into his bed (they had twin beds, afraid that at their ages sleeping-habits would not be compatible) without waking Annalee.

Janie was still in his thoughts. He'd shared one large bed with her.

Guilt-ridden Janie wanted to punish herself, and to show off in public. "Look, I've got a deaf-mute child! And I can sign!" So could her parents. He knew each time they were discussing him, pointing at him and not translating their comments into words. Any man would get paranoid.

But he loved Nicky more than Janie or her parents did, for love is demonstrated by self-sacrifice. Taking the easy way out was ruining Nicky. That's what Alan Teague said.

Ironic. The Katzes refused to turn Nicky over to him for the remaining three weeks unless he found an "interpreter" to live here or visit every day. He agreed. He would have agreed to anything. Annalee got cracking, and located an educated deaf man who could talk. A model for Nicky when he grew up.

With a new husband in her house, and three difficult teenagers, surely Janie could be persuaded to give up Nicky. Give over custody. "Leave Nicky with me, permanently," he told the Janie who stood there invisible. "Nine years with you, now give him the next nine years with me. He'll over-stress your new marriage. He sure meant the end of ours. Give him to me. I love him more than you do."

Nicky

How could he get back to Pittsburgh?

Pittsburgh is in Pennsylvania. Mama was in Japan. She'd taken him to Grandma and Grandpa, who were smart but got tired and sick. "Hush, hush," they signed, and took long naps when he wanted to do something. He was never sure when he was being quiet.

If only he'd been able to stay home in Pittsburgh with Kirby and Leah and Elyse, but Mama said they were too young to take care of him. They should all run away together and make Mama cry. She'd found someone she liked much better than them. They could go west and ride horses on a ranch.

It was fun, he admitted, when Grandpa read Nature books to him, and Grandma told him about Pilgrims and Puritans and frowned "Ugh!" when Grandpa cut up the frog.

Other kids didn't see inside frogs til tenth grade, but he saw what was in there at nine years old. In a big book they read about amphibians losing tails and wigglers in the water so little they're called "minute," which doesn't mean sixty-in-an-hour, and doesn't speech-read the same, either.

Mama was horrible to get married. He scowled and kept scowling, because his feet felt like bare on hot pavement. His sisters walked slowly in the wedding with fancy dresses, but he said no, he wouldn't carry the ring.

They'd shown him Japan on the globe he got at Christmas. Mama would stand upside down in Japan. Steve's boss, they said, had business with Japan, so they'd ride on a boat. Go away for weeks and weeks. Nicky said, "Don't come back."

It was their honeymoon. He never saw the word "honeymoon" without thinking how the sun was more like honey than the moon.

Steve used to write him notes, or Nicky flipped his eyes past Steve to see words in the air that Steve was saying through his bushy mustache.

"Please trim your mustache!" Leah said. "Nicky can't read just one lip!"

(Daddy didn't have a mustache, but Daddy's lips didn't move much.)

Everyone laughed at Steve, even Nicky. He liked to laugh with people, not just look up from food or game to see everyone laughing and never know why. Steve played real rough and threw him up in the air and said he liked boys, but after he took Mama away, Kirby said, "I bet he won't act any better with Nicky than Dad did."

Nicky had felt like crying. Steve had promised, and Daddy never promised. Were they all alike, Daddys? Steve had a "sense of humor," Elyse spelled on her hand. Daddy didn't. Nothing Nicky did when he came here seemed funny to Daddy. He always looked like going to cry or be mad, and his forehead was all wrinkled, and his mouth sad. Sometimes he looked old as Grandpa Katz. Mama said Daddy sold machines like typewriters and adders, and was smart, but he didn't act smart. You'd think Daddy couldn't even read, the way he hated any writing.

Nicky read a lot. There was nothing else to do in Tennessee. He'd tried to find kids' books here, and one was called *The Little Prince*. He liked that one, but the book with pigs on it, called *Animal Farm*, was hard. He liked *National Geographic*. The dictionary he found was hard, too, with little tiny print and lots of meanings for each word. How could he pick the right one? Long words aren't bad, usually, but the little ones play tricks, like "run" can be "run away" or "run a fever," but "running into" a person or a tree are different. "Run down" was by car or by tired. His nose ran and so did Leah's sweater in the wash. "Difficult" meant only one thing, but "hard" meant rocks and tests and luck and times, and hard up, hard on, hard at, and hard for meant all different things.

"Idioms," they were called, but he called them "idiots."

He had to read. He couldn't play outside or meet any kids on this road. He missed Joan and Ed and the twins next door, and even the Pittsburgh postman. He missed Louis and Bev and Susie in Lexington. He missed school and the planetarium and trips to see cows, and the newspaper that they all wrote and Miss Taft mimeographed. His was the sports page.

Hearie kids at home learned signs from him, and had fun with teachers and parents. They showed him hearies' signs like for baseball and football and Peace and Victory, but Mama said don't ever use some of those other signs in front of people. He used them behind people.

He rested more now, and made a new hole in his belt with a nail he found on the sidewalk. The money was still in his pocket after a man bumped him and looked back and fluttered lips at Nicky. It was like the TV commercial when one man bumps another man and takes all his money. Kirby said the bumped man was sad because he didn't carry Traveler's Checks.

Mama showed him Traveler's Checks for Japan, good as money, and the checks all said, "Jane Bratt." Brat means a bad kid. He hated that word—that name. Okay for Steve, but not for Mama, and he'd sure never have "Bratt" written on his school papers, even if it was much easier to say.

Knoxville streets were full of hearies with floppy mouths like chewing, and sleepy eyes. He put his head down and tried to look hearie by keeping his eyes half shut, too, and hoped no one else would bump into him and make his heart jump out.

When he wasn't able to walk anymore, for starving, he found a candy-machine in a gas station. He used the restroom and drank a gallon of water out of the sink faucet, and then waited til the man ran in to get his credit-card thing. Nicky held up his ten-dollar bill and pointed to the machine. making a trouble-face.

"Flutter-flutter," said the man (or he might be chewing gum), and ran outside to the car again. When he came back, he made change for Nicky, fast, because another car was coming in. He didn't look suspicious.

Now Nicky had lots of coins and bills. He decided on a chocolate bar and mints, and then a bag of peanuts, because Kirby said don't eat all sweets, you'll rot your teeth and bones. He put coins in too fast and had to do it over again, touching the machine to tell when each coin fell down. Hearies can hear that happen and always get their candy the first try.

He ate very fast, and felt a little sick. Nau-se-ate-ed. He didn't know where to go, or who could help him. He had only nine dollars and some cents left. It was getting hotter, and nobody looked at him. He saw a cop and ought to ask for help, like Mama said to do when in trouble, but he didn't dare. He'd have to go right back to Daddy and the lady who maybe was Daddy's sister or cousin. She was bigger and softer than Mama, and hugged nice, but she was stupid about signs and cried a lot. Worst of all was crazy man who came every afternoon and hurt and hated him.

If he had to live here any longer, he'd die. He didn't want to die. He wasn't even ten years old.

On TV he saw a story with a boy so sad he jumped off a bridge. Another time a lady jumped in front of a train. Or they put a rope around neck and then cowboys hit the horse, horse runs, and you swing and swing and are hanged. He thought about that. It made him feel like crying, but he kept thinking about all the ways to make yourself dead.

Lanier

Morning, already? Lanier stretched, turned over, rubbed his bristling chin and checked his Chronograph. The alarm hadn't sounded this Saturday morning, nor had Nicky, either. Often Nicky woke them by pounding on his door.

Interesting to see Nicky sleep so late after going to bed early for once. He hadn't sat up glaring at the TV last night, at shows he couldn't understand, pouting with his mouth drawn down.

"You don't have a TV closed-captioning system," Charlotte Katz had said to him over the phone. "Nicky depends on that for his television viewing. I should think any electronics expert with a deaf child could manage to obtain–"

And he broke in, promised to get one. Subtitles from a box. Promise them anything. Bones to the dogs. Dogs? They'd made a monkey out of his son. Janie had.

Scientists were using sign language with apes, when Janie took it up. He'd come home one day to find his wife talking to eighteen-month-old, just-diagnosed Nicky on her fingers. When Bob, at the store last year, pinned up a photo of a chimp busy at one of the brands of computers they carried, grinning pink gums and wrapping prehensile toes around the machine, Lanier didn't laugh.

Janie's father had telephoned yesterday to tell him his former mother-in-law was out of the hospital now, but Nicky could stay on in Tennessee if he was doing well. Since the child couldn't speak on the phone, Daddy gave them reassurances. Then he phoned his other children in Pittsburgh, left alone to survive for a month, the eldest only eighteen. Janie claimed that neighbors on both sides would check on them daily, but Lanier asked them about the sleep they were getting, their diets, and their summer jobs. The real questions one could not vocalize: "Are you snorting cocaine or shooting up heroin? Getting yourselves or someone else pregnant?" There was nothing he could do about it, short of driving or flying up there to see them.

"Keep Nicky," he told himself. "Don't let Stephen Bratt have him."

Suppose one day he discovered his son's name had been changed? No, no, no! Start Annalee out with a beautiful, almost perfect son almost ten, right for her age of thirty-two. With three in the family, Annalee had begun to cook fabulous meals, and though they had such different tastes in food, music and books, she'd labored over Nicky, talked and talked to him, made the child look at her lips, and she had obtained their required expert, as well.

Annalee's girlfriend at Sundew Florists knew a person who'd met a talking deaf man. Alan Teague, a computer programmer for TVA, no less, had once been just like Nicky. He understood exactly what had gone wrong, and why. He'd met others like Janie; nowadays there were more and more of them.

Lanier slipped back to sleep nestled in his dream of Nicky growing up to be another Alan Teague—a tall, handsome man with a well-paying position, normal people for friends, and no need for hand-motions to make people stare. No peddling alphabet cards for Nicky. No deaf wife (that Janie promised he'd marry), no deaf world. The hearing world. He was willing to support Nicky all the rest of his life, to save him from humiliation.

At nine-thirty he awoke again. Saturday, and he'd earned a morning in bed. Not a sound yet from Nicky. Annalee was in the shower; he could hear water running, and there was no shapely series of bulges under her pink floral sheets. She, too, liked to wait upstairs til the furious banging began.

"I musn't lose a second wife because of Nicky," he thought, and put that notion away. What had Alan said? Nicky did things to make you think him normal. He'd pick up a book or magazine and move his eyes back and forth across the page, pretending to read material too advanced for any born-deaf child, said Alan. He'd sit on the stereo speakers, swinging his feet, pretending to hear music.

Alan agreed with the experts. Mutism is archaic, like leprosy and polio. Modern technology makes it an unneccesary affliction. Thus far, only Nicky's spoken intonation distinguished question from demand. His vowels went up and down, and only "No!" was clear. He said "No!" a lot. As for Alan, he could talk to anyone and usually make himself understood. He lipread, often without asking you to repeat. Alan called himself "oral," and Nicky "manual."

"Nicky," he murmured, as he rose out of bed, "Today may be a turning point. For once you've gotten a full night's sleep, and let us enjoy one, too. Let the words come flowing out that we've poured into your eyes, if not your ears. Give Annalee something back for all her efforts. Your lips move so well for the words I presume you are saying.

"Just say them, darn it!"

He was admiring Annalee's silhouette through the shower screen, when she called out to him from under water, "Remember my beauty shop appointment this morning, honey."

So he'd stay home alone with Nicky until afternoon. Fine. Father and son, man to man. No possibility of a daytime sitter, unless Alan came early. They hadn't asked him to sit at night, and no one else possibly could handle Nicky. Annalee had earned a dinner out.

After his own shower, he dressed and stowed yesterday's clothes in the hamper. No more littered floors; he was again a thoughtful husband.

He went downstairs. Nicky still slept. Miraculous! Maybe he'd be in the mood to be taught something. Could Nicky read? Do math? He did try to write, but Alan said never let him take an easy way out. "How can you expect him to read or write before spoken language? all of us talked before becoming literate."

He slid the chair out from under the doorknob, opened the door, and looked in on Nicky. Warm this morning, but the child was still bundled up and asleep. Give him another half hour, and then bring him a Strathgordon Special, a whipped fruit drink he'd invented during bachelorhood. Nicky liked those.

In the kitchen he poured a cup each of cherry yogurt and cottage cheese into the blender, added two bananas, milk, and half a packet of cherry gelatin. He stood and watched the mixture puree. Once he tried to add a marshmallow, which made such a crash he might've tossed into the whirring blender a size AA battery. Amazing, but how would you explain a noisy marshmallow to Nicky?

Lanier downed his own glassful and kept the rest in the blender for Nicky. With toast. He'd fix him toast and an egg, and sit and watch the child eat.

Then he'd direct Nicky to the bathroom, and say, "Bath, bath," turning on the water for emphasis. He'd sit and watch Nicky undress, the small naked golden body velvety with pale down.

Nicky planted his feet so firmly that his knees curved backwards. The stubborn little jaw and large eyes meant he'd be a handsome man. Like Alan. Maybe as tall as Alan, who was taller than Lanier.

Nicky rejected help with buttoning up and shoe-tying, and Lanier knew he shouldn't insult the child by offering to aid him. What all could he do? He'd asked Kirby, but Nicky's brother was at the shrugging age. He could almost hear him shrug over the telephone.

It was silly not to wake Nicky. He might be ill. Or dead. That idea jarred him toward Nicky's room. Fast. He crossed the rug, put on a smile, put out his hand to touch the little brown head, half-covered and still. This morning Nicky wasn't signing to himself in his sleep and smiling as he sometimes did.

The head was cold, and hollow. Like plastic.

Which it was.

Lanier whipped off the covers. The big astronaut doll lay in Nicky's bed, and Nicky was gone.

Gone from his bed, gone from the confines of the toy-filled bedroom. Lanier ransacked it, until he saw that the window stood open, without its screen.

He wanted to roar, to scream, to curse, but he made himself search the whole house, pretending that Nicky was only teasing, hiding. He'd been sly enough to slip back into the house. But the doors were all securely locked.

By eleven, he was frantic. Annalee wasn't reachable by phone, and his control was going. His hands shook. Why hadn't he put Nicky upstairs near them, instead of downstairs in the sunniest, brightest room? Why not touch him last night? Touch that fake Nicky—that spaceman.

Then he remembered the dogs. At two a.m. dogs were barking, close by and then further and further away, in the direction of the city-center. Was that Nicky? Had a dog attacked him? Dogs can kill small children, and a deaf child would not hear a ferocious mastiff snarling.

The boy was gone. He'd pried up a window his father had trouble pulling back down again, and dropped onto a four-step ladder hidden in the bushes. Or someone had stood on the ladder to climb in and steal him. Kidnap him. The Lindbergh baby had been stolen from an upstairs nursery by a man with a long, long ladder. Lanier felt like vomiting, and drank some water, which didn't help.

Nicky must still be in pajamas. There were no discarded pajamas in view anywhere, even under the bed—where the window screen was hidden. That gave him hope. Would a kidnapper bother to hide the screen, once the boy was gone?

When had he left? This morning at two? Dogs did not bark at a car with kidnapper and child. Nicky was tiny, penniless, deaf, and mute. On foot?

He made forays to neighbors' houses among grassy hills under willows and sour gums, asking if a deaf child had moved in with anyone.

No, no such child had been seen. He saw pity in the faces of the well-fixed professional men's wives on their way to the golf course or polishing parquet floors. There was also visible their suspicion that his "handicapped" child had reason to run away. He hadn't lived here long; he hadn't met any of them before. What an introduction.

He wanted to shout that he was not a bad parent. He'd never beaten his son, never even had him to himself overnight, until now. He blushed when one woman asked, "Does Nicky run away often, Mr. Strassgordon?"

Nice people in nice houses like the one he'd bought for Annalee and meant as a home for Nicky as well. Now he must call the police, and pray that they'd find Nicky, that they'd found him already.

Alive.

He rushed back to the house, silently begging Nicky to come back, relent, come out of hiding and spare him this terror. What if he'd run away and been picked up on the road by some vicious pervert?

"Oh, my God!" he cried, skidded to the phone, and dialed the police.

They arrived within ten minutes and took only five more to find pajamas rammed into the foot of Nicky's bed. He'd changed clothes under the covers, they suggested. (Who had taught him that?)

"Keep calm, Mr. Strathgordon," one officer drawled. "This is a real nice, rural area. It's not likely he's gone far or gotten himself hurt."

"My little son is deaf and dumb!" Lanier told them.

"That's real unfortunate," the policeman replied, his face drawn down. "That'll make him a trifle harder to find, I reckon. And harder on you, to wait til he's found."

He patted Lanier's shoulder. "Real sorry to hear he's an unfortunate, but they do wonders nowadays, Mr. Strathgordon, for the handicapped."

Marti

Marti Hanson drove out of The Great Smoky Mountains National Park, down from heights where she'd watched the evening sun descend behind ridge after ridge of jagged black evergreens, relieved by heath-balds and groves of paler deciduous trees. Because she'd loitered, she'd arrive late at night in Knoxville.

Night-driving was a no-no. She practically had to rest her chin on top of the steering wheel, peering through her glasses like Mr. Magoo. Reflections off windshield and lenses gave her eyestrain—a strain shared by her passengers—but the passenger tonight was only Hildegaard, her huge mongrel pup. Hildie, with ears nearly touching the truck roof, a tall, snub-nosed, leggy dog, rolled white eyeballs at Marti.

"Relax, Hildie." she said. "I can manage to get us home. It's not eleven, yet, and there's a moon."

She wanted coffee, though, to reawaken her, so she halted beside a cafe on Magnolia Avenue, blinking away the afterglow of headlights, street lights, and neon. She climbed down from her pickup-plus-camper, and Hildie took the driver's seat and sighed.

"Back soon. Bring you a cracker."

The cafe was straight out of her childhood memories: highly polished wooden floor, pillars, round tables under white cloths, surrounded by wicker-backed chairs. Did Indianapolis any longer claim such institutions? The room was filled with the fragrance of ham and sweet potatoes, though truck-drivers must have finished late suppers hours ago. A fern on the windowsill by her table dangled fronds over her coffee cup.

The coffee was good, gentled with cream and sugar. By the time she finished, complimenting herself for the will-power to refuse both pecan and lemon meringue pie, she began to wonder about a lonely little boy sitting across the empty room.

He'd come in after she did, and stolidly plunked himself down at a table. When the waitress asked what he wanted, he pointed to the menu. Receiving a hamburger, he consumed it in what seemed three bites, and now was carefully wiping his fingers and mouth with a napkin.

A nice, mannerly little boy, she admitted, though he represented the shrieking, clamoring age that always appalled her. Blessed with any brothers , she'd have a thicker skin, but she was an only child, a lonely-only; kids in general scared her. She warmed up to them slowly, preferably one at a time. Preferably little girls, or boys over twelve.

He looked only about seven, and it was how late? Eleven. The toes of his sneakers scarcely touched the floor, and he wore jeans and a blue shirt with the sleeves rolled up. Brown hair hung down almost into his eyes, which darted glances around the room with a sort of intent, anxious look Marti found endearing. Walt Disney, where are you? He was perfect for some G-rated animal-film, a boy to frolic with calves and collies. Such an intelligent-looking, delicate child is not the sort who wanders around at night stealing hubcaps.

When the waitress came back to ask if the boy wanted anything else, he gave her a suspicious look and a head-shake. Then he studied the check, dug for a fistful of cash, and levered himself out of the chair, one arm braced on the table. When his feet struck the floor, he winced. Marti noted that, and wondered if he had an injury. She was familiar with runners' injuries. Or was he perhaps a beaten child?

She sat up straighter, studying him. He certainly looked miserable enough to be in some sort of trouble. He had to pass her table on his way to the cash-register, so she leaned toward him and whispered, "Hey, Honey, aren't you out pretty late at night?"

He cut her cold.

Marti blinked.

Hey, wait a minute, kid! I just asked you one reasonable little question!

She made a quick assessment of herself: sweater, jeans, a bandanna over bobbed, brown hair. She'd made more than one child ask, "Are you a kid, or a Mama?" because she moved like a teenager—thanks to jogging—but this year she'd turned thirty. Unmarried. To most of her southern friends a spinster, to Yankees an envied bachelorette on wheels.

Did the little boy know that kids scared her, that she could see herself someday mothering foreign orphans or homeless foster children, but not handling a breakable infant? Of course he didn't. He was just plain rude.

Or over-tired. Or scared.

She stood up, took two steps in pursuit of him, and grabbed his arm.

Pivoting, the boy sent her a horrified grimace, tore free, threw his money onto the counter by the register, and bolted through the door.

Marti retreated to her table, picked up a packet of crackers for Hildie, and stood there puzzled, in boots still damp from mountain streams. The boy's little arm was so icy. He needed a sweater.

She paid her own bill, smiled at the sleepy waitress, and went out into the dark to find her pickup.

She didn't expect to see the boy ever again.

Rolling out into the traffic on Magnolia, pretty sure she headed in the right direction, but promising herself an automobile compass to aid in navigation, she didn't even look for him.

But there he was.

The little boy was trudging down the street in the direction she was going, walking with arms crossed over his chest, illuminated by one car's headlights and then another's. He looked very forlorn. She crept along the curb in second gear, letting other cars past.

He didn't go into any of the houses, and now she could see how badly he was limping.

Marti geared up to third, biting her lower lip. Hildegaard, crackers on her breath, nosed her in the ear and gazed where she was gazing. Well ahead of the boy, Marti pulled over, killed the engine, and left her truck and dog. She crossed the street and stood in the middle of his sidewalk, so when he came walking along in the dark, he almost bumped into her.

He let out a God-awful cry of surprise as she crouched and anchored him still.

You ARE lost, aren't you? What's your name and address? You realize how late it is? Tell me where you live. Do you know your telephone number?"

Too much. He just stood there, refusing to answer.

Autistic? What's it called, autistic, or aphasic? He didn't resist when she drew him against her and lifted him, finding the child surprisingly light for her hundred-twelve to carry across the street. She put him in the seat beside Hildegaard, and when he leaned against the wagging, whining dog, he struggled and cried out again. He almost slid past her under the steering wheel.

"Whoa!" she cried. "Hildie's an angel! She won't bite, she'll just kiss you to death."

Marti climbed up under the wheel, while Hildie wash-ragged the boy's face as he sat pinned between the two of them. His tears were all wiped away. Marti turned on the engine and the heater, and rubbed a pair of cold little arms til the boy stopped shuddering. She unrolled his sleeves down to his wrists, wondering why he'd rolled them up so high, and then found one sleeve was badly torn. Odd. Was he so concerned about appearance as that?

Suddenly the boy pushed his face between her breasts, clung to her, and began to sob.

Nicky

Nicky raised his head when the truck stopped moving, and the lady from the restaurant moved. He waited for her hands to come down and prop him up against the big, soft dog; he was too tired, leaning against them both, to sit up without folding in the middle. It was a nice dog, not biting you.

Night, his second night, and he didn't care where she took him, because he didn't know what to do. He couldn't find the Greyhound buses, and his money went fast for food. The hamburger saved his stomach, but not his legs or his head. They kept fading away. Now for the first time he knew what Grandma meant, saying, "I'm so tired, I just can't wait to get to bed."

The lady leaned over him and ruffled his hair like all ladies do, and suddenly he remembered something.

When Grandma Strathgordon died, Grandma Katz told him people always leave behind other people to look after kids. He still had grandparents and Mama. He asked what if his grandparents died, and then Mama died, but she was young, so they said she wouldn't. But he'd seen plenty in the paper about young people dying, and he asked what if she got cancer or got run over. Grandma said there'd be another nice lady to look after him; she didn't know who, but God would send him one. She promised that from up in heaven, all of them would make sure he was taken care of.

He wondered if Mama died in Japan, and this lady was sent from her. (Can you get to heaven from Japan?) This lady felt like Mama and looked like her, too, in pants and a scarf on hair and a sweater and holding you tight. If Mama wasn't dead, why hadn't she come back and taken him away from Daddy?

It got all mixed up in his head. Mama was dead, or Mama was mean. She'd left and would never come back. For sure she hated him. Or she was in heaven?

The lady picked him up, and he laid his head on her shoulder as she carried him to a house. She put him down on his feet on the doorstep. His legs didn't hold him, so he hung onto the big dog's back that came up under his arms. She opened the door and lifted him inside and carried him under the arms, hanging, over to a green sofa.

He sank into it, face-down, without moving one finger, even to find out if she knew signs. She took off his shoes and socks, and felt his feet, kneeling by him in her jeans and bending her head with short brown hair and big glasses and blue eyes when he peeked at her. He hadn't seen any toys around, or a daddy.

That's all he noticed before he sighed and sighed, and under the thick, fuzzy blanket she put over him, went softly off to sleep.

Marti

Marti made herself a cup of instant cocoa and sat in the recliner chair. She'd turned out every light but the green-shaded lamp on the nearest end-table, enough to let her watch the little boy sleep. Nearly midnight, and she was wide awake from coffee and child-rescue. She ought to be on the phone to the police, but first she needed to plan what on earth to say.

She postponed digging out Susan's phone directory from the cobbler's bench beneath the inconvenient wall-phone. The phone in Susan's and Bill's bedroom would be better, less likely to disturb the kid. She tried to keep the cup and saucer from clinking, but children, they say, can sleep through anything. She didn't relish the idea of awakening a child who was sleeping like death and had somehow blistered his feet. She ought to put something on those blisters.

"Imagine!" she told herself. "Me, playing mommy, when I don't know beans about kids, and I'm a little old to start learning, solo."

She felt an urge to consult someone less formidable than the Knoxville police, but at midnight, only her parents in Indianapolis would welcome a phone call. She knew no one in town but the owners of this house—and her cousin Sue and husband were vacationing in New York. What about Mike Curran in Columbus? Call him and ask what he thinks about: first, that four-year-old girl as a fellow-competitor in his next marathon race, and second, a kid twice that age who was sleeping all blistered on her couch. "Maybe this kid just FINISHED a marathon," she mused.

Someone had washed the kid's little blue shirt and his sneakers, though. He belonged somewhere to someone, and somewhen, she'd better send him back. But he wasn't return-addressed. No name-label in his clothes.

She put a throw-pillow against the arm of the room's second sofa and lay down for a minute. Her eyelids drooped. Sleep was as contagious as a yawn. The boy had snuggled down between blanket and pillow so only his tightly shut eyes were visible, under the mass of brown hair.

Marti forced herself to sit up again, afraid she'd doze. Okay. Leave the decision to the kid himself. If he awakened, she'd learn who he was, and where he came from. If he confessed to being beaten, she'd sure call the cops. If he liked his parents, she'd call them. But he'd have to tell her who they were. He should be rested enough, soon, to be able to say something coherent. If he was still all blunked out, she'd have to resort to the police. Eventually.

If he were running away from bad parents, the longer they missed him and suffered, the better, she told herself. Parents? Be realistic. It's almost fifty-fifty that a kid in trouble has no father, nowadays.

She called out, "Hey, kiddie! Son? Hey, you'd better wake up and talk to me, now."

She waited, leaning forward. He didn't stir.

"You really need sleep, don't you?"

She said that much louder, and held her breath. Not a lash flickered. Again, she inquired about his preferences, but he didn't move.

Marti shrugged. Okay. Let's see if cousin Sue lists the local police in the front of her phone book, or do I have to go through all the city and county listings? Which shall it be, city cops or highway patrol? She'd snatched him off the highway. In this city.

"Brother, I'm done in, myself," she admitted. "I'd better put the percolator on before the law arrives!"

Nicky

When Nicky woke up, it wasn't day. The lamp was bright in his eyes, and there wasn't a lady touching him, now, but a man.

He opened his eyes wide, on a big, new face. Not Daddy's. Right near his face it said something, smiling. The man's shirt was gray and stiff, and labels were on it, like he was a cop. Nicky looked over the edge of the sofa where the man was crouching down, and saw the holster and the big pistol. Was it a Colt 45?

The policeman sat Nicky up on the couch with his legs stuck out in front of him, all the time making flutter-lips. The lady in glasses came and sat sideways on the sofa, flutter-fluttering her lips and combing his hair with a pink comb. The policeman took out a notebook and wrote in it, and now the lady's hand held a photograph of Nicky just like one they took of him last year in Lynnwood School.

Nicky watched the policeman write. He wanted to grab the pen and write things he needed to say, but he might get shot. Cops shoot people who don't hear cops say, "Stop, or I'll shoot."

The cop would call Daddy, he bet. He hadn't even gotten out of Knoxville, or found Greyhound or a signer, or any store that said, "Sign Language Spoken Here," in words and hands.

Flutter-flutter, their mouths went, with lots of "cows," or maybe "hows" and "nows." Another cop came into sight behind the sofa, and Nicky spelled a quick "H" and "I" to him to see if maybe he was smart, because he was younger, but he wasn't. He didn't know what Nicky said.

The old cop unfolded his legs and got up and went to the telephone. Nicky wanted to say, "Don't do that!" but he had to sit still and watch. The cop put the notebook under his arm and dialed. The lady ran away and came back smiling. She handed Nicky a big chocolate-chip cookie in a paper napkin, and the room started to smell like coffee. She kissed him again, and he was glad she didn't wear lipstick. He tried to think of everything except Daddy coming. She had little wrinkles around her eyes under the glasses, like Mama. He tried, with his free hand, to finger-spell a few words to her, but she didn't read them. She moved her lips very slowly now, and opened her mouth wider, so he knew she'd figured it out. That he was deaf.

Nicky watched the policeman's face while he talked on the phone. The man's eyes came over to him, while his lips went faster, and he nodded. Nicky was afraid the cookie would come back up, but when he choked, the lady ran away and came back with a glass of milk. He poured that down his throat, fast, on top of the cookie inside him to keep it down.

The cop was surely talking to Daddy, and Nicky was caught.

Lanier

Lanier ran from the telephone into the bathroom to comb his hair, but did a messy job of it. Nicholas was safe, in some woman's house in east Knoxville, with two policemen to guard him. Thanks be to heaven!

He was red-eyed from sitting up all night by the phone, and Annalee wasn't back yet from the TV station. She'd broadcast, live, an appeal to any kidnapper who might have Nicky. They calculated that a mother (never mind the "step-") would inspire more pity than Nicky's father. Annalee loved doing it, but it meant she wasn't here either to find Nicky missing, or to learn he was safe.

Twenty-four hours since Nicky vanished, but Nicky was all right! He wished he could stop trembling and panting like a winded athlete. "He's okay. He's okay!"

He drove over the speed limit to the address he was given. Nicky could have been brought straight home; the police offered that service, but Lanier was desperate to get out of the damned prison of the house and meet the woman who'd found him. How could they be sure she hadn't harmed him?

Nicky's journey was a total mystery he had to clear up.

Inside the modest frame house with a police car out front to signify he had the address right, Lanier looked for his son. Nicky did not come running to greet him.

The child sat on a couch hugging a big stuffed frog, and when Lanier hastened over and knelt to hold him, Nicky groaned (horribly) and turned away, trying to slide behind a bespectacled young woman in jeans who had the grace to look embarrassed. She'd picked him up outside a restaurant where Nicky had purchased dinner. With what? Five dollars was found by the police in Nicky's pocket. Whose money?

Lanier's explanation that Nicky's mother was in Japan and he had been given the opportunity to teach his deaf son speech obviously impressed the girl and the policemen. They'd had a devil of a time themselves, trying to communicate with Nicky.

Nicky was not moving, glaring at his father with nothing less than dread. Lanier borrowed a sheet of paper from the girl and held it, with a pencil, toward Nicky. after he'd written at the top, "Where were you? Why?"

Nicky turned away his head and wouldn't touch it.

After the police paperwork was finished, he picked up a very limp and silent Nicky to carry like a sack of laundry out to his car. The girl offered to ride along, "to hold Nicky." She could return home in a cab, she added.

Because she didn't say, "Nicky might try to jump out of the car," he answered, "Yes, thank you." Thanks for your tact.

She wasn't a girl anymore, he saw on a closer look, but she was slim and small and soft-spoken, obviously educated. In her demeanor he glimpsed potential as a babysitter. She was single, she said, childless, and unoccupied for this week of house-sitting.

He told her about Janie and Annalee as he drove the dawn-empty dark streets. Nicky sat on her lap, facing away from him, pouting. Where had he been for all those hours? When, exactly, had he left? Did he have help? Did he escape a kidnapper? One sleeve was torn from elbow to cuff, flapping open. Lord knows how he'd done that, but there wasn't a cut or bruise on him for the police to find. The girl had doctored Nicky's blistered feet, and he wore, instead of his own shoes, a pair of her thick wool socks. And one of her sweaters.

No way to ask Nicky where he'd been; he was sealed tight.

"He's had no father for six years. He's not only mute, he's also a Mama's boy," Lanier said. "I've recently remarried. We'll fight for custody, now, my wife Annalee and I."

"So few fathers get their children. It's not at all fair," she immediately responded.

"Nicky, if you can believe it, attends a school with deaf-mutes as teachers," he said.

"ALL of them are deaf-mutes?"

"Not all, but many. Isn't that appalling?"

When they ascended the long, sloping driveway, Annalee was already outside, lights blazing in the windows behind her. She must've heard. The return of the Prodigal Son. (Lanier wondered if she'd had time to prepare a feast, kill the Fatted Calf.) Annalee didn't hesitate to fling open Marti's door and embrace both her and the child, chattering and weeping.

When he got both women inside he poured each of them a mis-made drink. Nicky wouldn't come to him or to Annalee, or even look at either of them. Marti tried to extricate herself from Nicky's embrace, while all of them talked loudly to cover the awkward dilemma of a child ungrateful to be home safe.

"This is such a lovely room!" Marti Hanson exclaimed.

It was. His family-room-kitchen sported a huge free-stone fireplace, a copper-topped stone range, and natural pine furniture. It was draped in Creeping Charlie and Wandering Jew. A big brick house, under ivy, with plank doors and white windowframes—just what he'd always wanted. The room they occupied was strewn with toys, but Nicky ignored them, finally sinking into the rug in front of the TV, watching with the sound off.

Exhaustion suddenly hit Lanier, left him half-reclining, boneless, in one corner of the couch, while Annalee and Marti sat knee-to-knee at the other end, discussing Knoxville.

Over there lay his beautiful child, so unlike the twisted, limbless little creatures featured on coin-cans at check-out counters. "It's invisible," he thought. "His affliction is so invisible." Nicky's rescuer had been totally flabbergasted to hear he was deaf. She'd never suspected.

"Maybe jogging would wear Nicky out, so he'd be easier to handle," he put in, when Marti described her peculiar occupation. "Maybe before you leave town you could come over and jog with him. Give us a chance to get out for one evening."

"I'd love to," she said. (Brave girl. She must see that he and Annalee were burned out.)

"But his feet need a week to heal," Marti added.

They settled on a day and hour. This Tuesday evening at five, Marti could cook Nicky's supper and babysit. Nicky knew her already; he'd be manageable, corrigible (as opposed to incorrigible). She'd be supportive of their efforts. She promised, nodding, smiling, eager. Not eager so much for pay, but to help. Or so he assumed.

Annalee wouldn't know it, but Marti very much reminded Lanier of Janie. A Janie on his team for once; on his side.

Nicky

Nicky lay on the rug, chin in hand, afraid the nice lady would go away and leave him. Couldn't he return home with her, and stay til he could get to Pittsburgh? Maybe she'd drive him to Pittsburgh, in the truck with the dog, maybe tonight. He should write her a note to ask her to.

She knew he was deaf, but she didn't slap hands and say, "Talk, talk," when even the best deaf talkers make hearies frown and back slowly away. He pretended not to pay attention to Daddy, lady, and lady, but he watched them reflected in the TV screen. He didn't even have to turn his head.

All the way here he'd lain against his new lady. Talking, she felt like a big, purring cat. If only he'd written something for her. He should have woken up before the cop, and found paper and pencil at her house. She didn't have any little school desk like Daddy did.

The little desk made his stomach go "Yuk!" He had to sit for hours and hours with the fat lady who gave him candy when he said stupid little words she held up. The tall man at night slapped him, so once he threw up all over the desk and the man. The man left. Daddy cleaned him and then kissed him, but Nicky stayed mad. Someone old and big shouldn't be mean to a kid. That wasn't fair. And he didn't know if it would ever end, but running away only made him very, very tired.

He almost fell asleep over a show where nothing happened but people talking, then crying more than talking. He woke up to see an airplane on fire, falling red through the blue sky. It was real, no cartoon, so he turned around to the three hearies and pointed. They weren't even looking. He jumped up and pointed to the TV, and then he remembered the sound must still be off, and hearies need sounds like blind people do. So he ran and turned the knob all the way around. Daddy motioned to turn it down, down, down, pushing down with his hands in an almost-sign.

So Nicky turned it down.

The plane crashed and burned up.

Nicky thought of all those people in the plane. Poor people! Did they all burn up?

"A real plane-crash? Real people killed?" he asked in voice and signs. "A story, or true, real?"

They all looked unhappy, over there on the sofa with wrinkled brows.

"People, people, people all die?"

He signed it in English, clear to hearies, and tried hard with voice, but no one moved.

Then Daddy suddenly turned red in the face and made his mouth ugly and waved arms in the air. He swayed body and threw his hands and got redder. The ladies looked like hurting. Suddenly Nicky understood.

Daddy wasn't sick or crazy. Daddy was making fun of signs.

Nicky threw himself on mean, mean Daddy like a bomb exploding, and hit, hit, hit. He yelled loud as he could, every sound he knew, hoping to hurt ears. He spit out noises at mean, horrible Daddy. "Hate, hate, hate you!"

Daddy's mouth went fast; he held Nicky while he shook his head at the ladies. Fat lady reached for him, but when Daddy let go, Nicky fell toward his new lady, who hugged him and rocked him til he could breathe again. She was strong and smelled like trees, not flowers, so when he got a hand loose, he put his middle fingers down and the others and his thumb out and showed her what hearies like to sign. And she smiled.

He couldn't believe it, but she smiled, and her hand tried to make that same sign, too.

Daddy got red again, and flapped mouth like dog barking, and fat lady was white. Then Nicky speechread Daddy.

Because he wasn't trying to, he caught two clear words: ". . . dirty sign. . . ."

He screamed out loud, so they sure heard it, and kicked at Daddy, hard. He was stupid and mean. Why didn't he ever learn? Fat lady was crying. Heads went shake, shake. It wasn't dirty. Daddy was dirty! Nicky bit his teeth together so hard it hurt. He wanted to bite Daddy. He looked at his new lady with no name and made the sign again, I and L and Y all together, like hearies make "FBI."

Stupid hearies don't know one thing. One word. Or three. Nicky was sick of crying. His eyes hurt, but he lay on the rug and cried and didn't look at any of them anymore.

Marti

Marti woke the next morning to sharp memories of that pleasant newlywed couple trapped with their child out in the country. At least this man and wife loved each other, and worshipped little Nicky. Divorces among her friends scared her away from marriage, and she was sickened by breakups with neither spouse wanting custody of the kids. She only wished Mr. Strathgordon hadn't made fun of deaf language. A good thing she'd seen our nation's President, no less, hold up the handshape that means I-Love-You.

When she'd said the words to Nicky, on departing, just to check—the boy nodded fiercely and lipped them back to her, hiding the sign from Daddy.

She was surprised he lipread her. A good thing he didn't lipread his father, she thought. Had he realized Daddy considered the sign obscene, how doubly furious the boy would be, and justly so.

Annalee explained to her it's essential not to permit a deaf child signs. With gesturing as a way out, he'd never talk. All the books agreed, Annalee emphasized. For the first ten or twelve years, it was necessary to talk, talk, talk. He had, after all, to live in a hearing world.

Nicky, however, must feel awfully lonely, so she'd offered to lend them Hildegaard or one of Susan's three cats. They said they preferred he go it alone til Tuesday, when she'd babysit.

Embarassng to have Nicky favor her over his parents. Was that often true? Sacrifice for a kid, and he runs away and causes you agony and glombs onto a total stranger. She owed the Strathgordons sympathy.

Marti struggled out of bed, hunted for her glasses, and with glasses was able to locate her red caftan, and read the clock. Eleven-oh-five. She put the caftan on, put coffee on, and took out a jar of wheat germ. Before she allowed herself brunch, however, she placed a long-distance call to North Carolina.

A child named Kim Porter was hoping to take the marathon age-record away from a boy of four, Marti was told. At the Pine Mountain race she was . . . sort of catering. Yes, Kim supposedly had set her little heart on it. She'd run Pine Mountain on the ninth, and there was no way the marathon committee could prevent it.

It wasn't Marti's problem, but she sure sympathized. Why, marathoners over sixty worried her committee; a kid of four completely blew their minds. To smithereens.

Marti groaned. She sank down onto the couch to sit hugging her knees, bare toes hooked over the pillow-edge. Boy, oh boy! (Girl, oh, girl!) Her elderly volunteers at Pine Mountain had but one failing—their terror that something catastrophic would occur to ruin their marathon. "Think of the distance! Over twenty-six miles!"

"It'll rain!"

"Great!" she'd told them. "Most marathoners love to run in a gentle, warm rain." She didn't at first visualize elderly officials dealing with stop-watches, T-shirts, and ribbons while huddled under umbrellas.

"Someone will drop dead in our race!"

"Runners don't die in marathons," she told them. "Not a single one, ever, in the Boston Marathon, and very few elsewhere."

(And now, Kim Porter. They could hardly move the race out from under her. Why would a mother force a baby to run twenty-six miles?)

She'd sure gotten an education in the paraphenalia, feats, and fetishes of runners, from orthotics to fartleks to carbohydrate-loading. At the hometown Heart Association where she'd been assistant director, there were only two sins: cholesterol and sloth, so she swore off fat beef and started running. Voila! No longer a girl-pear!

"You've lost so much WEIGHT!" friends screamed, and no longer did it feel as if something was following her; what was following had been a little too much of her.

It started when a race-director fell ill and pulled her in to replace him. She next was talked into directing a new suburban marathon, and a career evolved. Luckily, her dad owned a shop selling customized T-shirts and trophies. These could be hand-delivered, along with her expertise, for a modest fee. She would lay out a course, gather volunteers, and direct a great, sweaty race complete with all the trappings. Motels and restaurants loved the crowds. She loved the excitement. Now she had bids for many races of ten miles and up, and instead of rent bought gas to drive all over the Midwest. She loved to drive, tax-deductibly.

There were backyards to park her camper in, and windows through which to poke her electric cord. In her camper was a big bed (over the truck-cab), a little desk, and a mini-bathroom. She needed no more.

Babysitting money from the Strathgordons would go toward much-needed new running shoes.

When she arrived at Nicky's house Tuesday at five, his parents were eager to depart. Nicky greeted her like a kid at Christmas, a note of near-hysteria added. He clawed her to him, hanging on, eyes desperate. He'd forgotton nothing. Out of sight of Lanier and Annalee, he flashed her I-Love-You.

She waited until after they left to make that one sign in return, and then mouth to him their dictum: "No more. You must learn to talk. No sign language; it's a hearing world, Nicky!"

She cooked chuck steak and rice and made them salads and an old fashioned sundae apiece, with chocolate syrup she found sitting way up on top of the refrigerator. He ate fairly well, watching her so intently she couldn't look at him. Before she got the table cleared, the boy vanished, and she found him, busily rummaging in her purse. This was intriguing, but all he dragged out of it was her ballpoint pen and an old grocery list. Rushing to the coffee table to kneel beside it, Nicky scribbled, "I like you. Take me home. I hate Daddy and everybody here." Then, while Marti watched over his shoulder, he inscribed an address and phone number.

Oh brother! She'd been strictly warned not to let the kid write notes. "Require speech," his father had commanded as they left, he looking younger in a neat gray suit beside his bride's slimming blue dress.

Nicky jerked the piece of paper nearer, to write, "I will teach you signs."

"Signs are not permitted," she wrote, then crossed that out, in favor of "Signs are a no-no."

(What was the vocabulary of a normal kid of nine? Not to mention a deaf one?)

Since she'd already sinned, she might as well compound it. She wrote, "Your daddy and step-mother help you. They love you very much."

He looked up at her, startled, pointing to the hyphenated word. Okay, a word too big for him.

"Daddy's new wife," she wrote. "New mama for you."

Nicky's astonished expression convinced her that he didn't even know his father and Annalee were married. In a week, they hadn't gotten that across to him? No wonder the child needed training!

Nicky suddenly snatched her hand in his and started manipulating her fingers.

"You rascal! Hey, no way!"

She took up her pen again and found space between "dog-food" and "watermelon" to write, "Writing is a no-no, too."

His face clouded over. He probably noticed she didn't look too delighted, either. Poor, frustrated little tyke! His vowel-laden voice was foggy and formless. She said, "I love you," because he could lipread that, and in response he said, "I run away with you, please? Please?"

Marti blinked. Was that what the sounds really meant? The shock of lipreading a whole sentence hit her. Had he noticed that she carried her living quarters on her truck, big enough for two? Maybe he also noted the running shoes she wore. Not that she was about to turn traitor to such nice parents as his .

The shrewd little rascal better watch out.

He poked her and said, ". . .understand me?" pointing to himself. She nodded yes, adding, "Do YOU understand ME?"

He returned a clear affirmative.

They'd certainly outdone his performance with Daddy and Step-mother, hadn't they? But when she tried asking, "Won't you learn? Why not? What is stopping you from talking?" Nicky shook his head.

"I don't . . . (something) . . . good," he said, shaking his head and making little finger-circles at his mouth. ". . . go with you. Please?"

Next the child made writing motions, but she shook her head no and balled up the paper. No, again.

He jumped off the sofa and ran to a cute little red school desk in the corner that looked brand-new. He sat down in it, grimaced, and then sprang up. From a rack near the sink, he obtained a flowered dishtowel, carried it back to the desk, and wound it around one wrist. He sat down, putting his wrist against the leg of the chair. When his other arm was similarly positioned on the other side, he pretended to tug and struggle.

Marti stared. What sort of game, of display? Then she understood. This was a charade. His face was vivid with despair. They'd TIED HIM UP? Tied him to the desk? Incredible. Could he concoct such a tale, though, if it bore no truth?

"Who? Why?" she asked, and he lipread the words and rushed to her, signing rapidly and confusingly. He pushed against her knees, saying "Ma– Ma–."

"Mama?" she echoed. But he corrected her. "Mahn! MAHN!"

Man. Not Daddy, then, or Annalee? Some man tied him up? Why? There had been mention of someone else, a man, a deaf male teacher. She covered both ears with her palms.

"Deaf? A deaf man tied you up?"

Nicky's jaw dropped. "DEAF?" he breathed, with the same astonishment as at "Daddy's new wife."

"Yes, a deaf man comes to teach you, right? But how could a deaf man teach you speech?"

Nicky drooped, unable to hold up his end of the conversation. Marti impulsively swept him into her lap, holding him very tight. For long minutes he remained cuddled against her, and she liked that. A far easier form of communication. When he wriggled free, he took her by the hand and led her into what must be his bedroom, with colorful elephant posters, and toys littering every surface. He led her straight to the window and pointed. Nails secured the window shut.

Her first response was to wonder if his room was awfully hot in the afternoons. Then she winced, not so much at the precaution but at the child's awareness of it. Why hadn't Nicky the escape-artist slipped out the front door, away from her? But he'd tried that already. He'd spent over twenty hours, hiking.

His feet were healed. She picked him up again to check.

But when she turned to leave his room, she stopped, startled. Against the wall stood an expensive-looking, four-foot plastic spaceman. In spite of its shiny newness, it was mutilated.

At the wrists, its hands had been crudely hacked off.

Marti didn't have to ask by whom. Or why. Her stomach reacted; it heaved as if she'd over-extended herself near a finish-line.

While she gloomily loaded the dishwasher, Nicky, in a furious pout, seated himself in front of the TV. No sound.

"Never again," she told herself, "will I feel the same way about a jabbering, even a whining child. A baby importunately tugging on Mama's sleeve, making its wishes clearly understood."

Moments later, she heard the little deaf-voice utter a cry.

She found Nicky kneeling close in front of the TV, staring so hard he didn't notice her arrival. She leaned around the set to discover what had captivated the boy.

A famous preacher was preaching.

Below him, in one corner, appeared an inset with a lady in black, spinning signs off her fingers.

Nicky lunged for the on-off button, covering it with both hands, saying rather clearly, "Not off, not off!"

She needed only two seconds to decide. Prying his hot little hands away from the knob, she didn't turn the set off. Instead, she turned up the sound, so she'd know what was going on.

Nicky sat frog-legged on the rug near the screen; he held that position and did not blink for half an hour.

Marti could not believe his concentration. He'd tuned in midway through the program, and it wasn't a sermon easy for a child. So far as she knew, he was totally ignorant of theology, but he sat there gazing, his hands no longer lying palm-up like a pair of murdered birds, but moving, opening and closing, as if he told himself what he was seeing.

Marti caught onto some signs, hearing the preacher and occasionally lipreading the interpreter. "Jesus" and "Bible" came again and again, and included touching the center of each palm with a fingertip.

"Nails!" she cried, pleased with her insight. "Bible" was nail-holes plus an opening book. A graceful sweep up and down of the hand above the face meant "God."

During the commercial, Nicky fidgeted, and Marti suffered remorse. But religion—after all! She didn't know what faith the Strathgordons professed, but any deaf kid who could sit through half a sermon—let him!

With the hymns, the signs came slower and were easier to guess. "Help" was lifting one hand with the other. "Ask" and "pray" used palms pressed together. "Soul" came wavering up out of the heart. She was almost tempted to imitate.

"Manualism," Nicky's father called this.

"Manual spaniel!" she said aloud. "Maybe Nicky got more from this than he ever got from his Daddy."

She understood the child's mournfulness when the program was over. Over. Gone. All gone. What had Nicky tried to ask the first night, when he was brought home? A late-late movie was on, and the child in a frenzy asked something no one understood, except it was a question. Daddy insulted him, and Nicky threw a tantrum.

She yearned to write Nicky another note, or invent some signs, but she dared not.

Diabetics mustn't eat sugar. Alcoholics mustn't drink whiskey. Same thing. Some things are poison to some people.

Nicky lay face-down on the rug, petulantly pulling at the shag loops til she feared he'd pluck it bald. Must she report all this to his parents? Did note-writing have to be included in her confession, or just the sermon? "We listened to–oops! We listened to and looked at a sermon on the need for foreign missions and for inter-racial harmony, and there just happened to be a bit of illegal signing down in the corner. . ."

She had a question to ask them, one too painful, she feared, to put to new acquaintances.

"Why did Nicky chop the hands off his plastic spaceman?"

Nicky

His I-Love-You lady went away. Nicky wrote for her his address and phone number in Pittsburgh, but he'd forgotten to put "Pittsburgh," and she didn't let him write any more. She said signs weren't permitted. Daddy wouldn't let her sign or write, which was so mean it made him cry again, lying in bed, remembering.

She'd let him watch the preacher, but she was scared. He could see scared in her eyes, and when Daddy came back, she was more scared. She told him Daddy was married to the fat lady. He'd thought maybe she was his aunt or cousin. No wonder she lived here, if she was wife like "housewife." Wife to this house. Daddy's house.

"Daddy ought to see the preacher say love everyone," he thought. The preacher said things like in the book he found at the stupid school.

It had been morning, days and days ago, and Step-mother dressed him nice, so he knew he was going somewhere. In the car they let him sit in back, alone, but watched him all the time in the rear-view mirror. He liked to go riding, but that was the only time he got to. They drove to a school, with swings in the yard, and he saw kids wearing hearing-aids like his.

But when he asked, "Do you like here? and "What games you play?" No one moved hands or mouth, just stared. He got mad at them. Stupid kids. They made ugly mouths and poked each other. He didn't see them understanding anything.

In the classroom, he picked up the book they were supposed to read, but it was a baby book like he had in first grade. Looking around, he saw most kids were bigger than him.

Lesson was silly. Make sound right, or you can't sit down again. He fast read the whole book. Stupid book about Farmer John and his animals. Half the class was standing up, waiting to make mouths again.

On the playground at recess, he stood away from the others, because they hit, hit, hit, instead of lining up or playing circle-games like at Lynnwood School. Teachers fluttered lips, but the kids didn't do much. Boring. No friends. No jokes.

In the Boy's Room after recess, he got a big surprise. Those kids that never moved hands were waving arms, now, like birds trying to fly, but he didn't see ideas or words on their hands. When he asked and asked—all the ways he knew—"What mean?" they just stared at him.

So he ran out and down the hall away, but a teacher caught him and dragged him back. That's when he tried to show he was in the wrong school. This must be an M.R. school. Or M.H. Multiple Handicaps. He grabbed a grown-up book off Teacher's desk, and opened it and read real fast and loud in signs and voice about prayers, til she took it away from him. One hard word was "justification," and he signed it in pieces to prove he could. Leah called that "showing off," but he had to. These were stupid kids, and he wasn't stupid. Mama said he was a Model Child. Kirby said he'd "get a Big Head" from that, so Nicky used to look in the mirror to see his head grow.

School wasn't as bad, though, as the tall crazy man who came. His Love-Lady told him the man was deaf. Crazy-deaf. Mean-deaf, worse than Daddy. For hours and hours, that man didn't even let him MOVE.

Deaf man held up cards with one word on them, for Nicky to say. "Bird." He was supposed to say "bird," and then "boy," and "baby." Daddy or Wife sat and listened. Deaf man couldn't hear. Couldn't teach, either. He'd hold a corner of a piece of paper by Nicky's lips to make him blow out air. Nicky knew how to blow. When he was two and three years old, teachers did that, and they'd say, "You're not a talking kind of kid," but that was okay. "Just try hard, hard, hard, because voice helps dumb hearies understand better."

Nicky groaned. His new lady who took him home with the dog was different. Nice. She wasn't smart, yet, but she could get smart. Kirby called people like that "open-heart." "-Ed." "Open-hearted." She had no name. Nobody here had names.

The bad deaf man made Nicky so sick, with flutter-flutter lips and slappings, that once Nicky screamed and signed and stood up inside the desk. His neck and mouth hurt. He grabbed the card that said "apple," and tore it up. The man didn't even draw a good apple.

Daddy and the man flapped mouths at each other, and Daddy went away. Nicky needed the toilet, but a "T"-hand wouldn't say that to them. His face got hot, and felt like it swelled up to a big red balloon. Daddy came back with sad face and two white handkerchiefs, one in each hand. The deaf man took them and knelt down by Nicky's desk. He pulled one of Nicky's hands down real quick and tied it to the chair; then he tied the other hand, too.

Nicky got sick, remembering. He'd screamed. His red balloon-head exploded in bright lights. He felt smothered. Daddy ran to him, but the man pushed him away. Step-mother came downstairs and made big mouth, O, and cried, but deaf man didn't even look.

Nicky was bouncing up and down in the seat, screaming, screaming, and throwing his head, "No, no, no, NO!" from side to side, so tears flew away.

The man stood holding onto Daddy til Nicky couldn't see them through tears squirting out of his eyes. He wet his pants like some baby. Bending over, he pounded his head on the desk til things got gray and spotted. Daddy and Step-mother were crying and holding on to each other. When the man went away, Daddy ran and untied him, and Step-mother tried to hug him, but he flew right up out of that desk and hit, hit,

hit. Hit them. That's when Daddy wrote him that first note. It said, "Teacher talks. His mother tied his hands when he was like you."

Then Daddy put him to bed with a pill.

Nicky cried from even thinking about it. The hairbrush on his hands had stung like fire, but this was worse. Tying hands he couldn't even think about. He would not stand for it. He would get away by running or by dying, because Mama was bad and gone, and they'd all be sorry if he was dead. He wanted to kill Daddy and Mama and maybe Step-mother, too, but maybe he would kill himself, instead.

Marti

Marti felt doubly disturbed by Nicky that night. After their return home, the Strathgordons failed to keep the pouting boy in bed. He wouldn't stay out of Marti's arms, and she refused to let them bar his door.

They made her a gin-sling so sugared that she didn't realize how much gin she was getting, and the effect on her tongue. Truth serum. Suddenly she heard herself describing the television episode and the note-writing, and even boasting of her ability to lipread Nicky.

"Sunday mornings someone translates sermons into gesture," Lanier said. "We dare not let Nicky watch. It will ruin him. I should have checked the *TV Guide* to see if in the evening–"

Her doubtful gaze sent him to another topic.

"I, too, have tried to lipread Nicky, but I cannot."

"Yet you expect him to lipread you?"

"Alan Teague's the one who ought to explain about Nicky," was Annalee's eager suggestion. "He is himself a deaf person. Being deaf himself from birth he can tell you what's what. You've got to meet him. He's a good-looking man, too."

"Nicky's teacher?"

"Every afternoon, after work. He's single—divorced—he's about your age; I think you two would just get along grand."

Marti glimpsed a wink that accompanied that last remark, but Lanier only frowned, then signed deeply. "We want you to sit again for Nicky, Marti," he said, "so please don't bend the rules. We depend on you as part of our support-team."

"I did what I felt was right at the time."

"Will you be busy Friday?" asked Annalee.

"You'd like me to sit again, so soon as that?"

"We need to go see our insurance man. You tell us if anything else comes up for Friday, okay?" she patted Marti's arm. "I think you're just great with Nicky. We need you so."

Marti got home on coffee and good luck, and went to bed depressed.

She'd told the truth. She was free between races and wasn't even in training herself for a ten-kilometer. Nicky's strange case kept her awake at night and in the daytime anxious. A real-life soap-opera, with Marti Hanson right on stage as one of the actors. A paid actor, in fact. Mr. Strathgordon—she felt odd calling him "Lanier"—paid very well. Lanier and Annalee. What a match. A sense of father and daughter, there, with Annalee (more comfortable to call her "Annalee" than "Mrs." Anything) the overfed, slightly spoiled, but good-hearted spinster daughter, staying home to take care of Papa. She wondered what Janie had been like, the first wife who was Nicky's mother. Annalee might be perfect for Nicky, with always a broad lap available and hugs and cookies. There had been two cookie jars, both full, three flavors of ice cream in the freezer, and a pan of fudge in the fridge.

As for herself, she felt disgustingly ignorant. So after her morning three-miler and her shower, she fed Hildegaard and the cats, ate a banana and a handful of peanuts and jumped into her sister's little Mazda. She took herself for a drive over the wide, pale green Tennessee River to "Island Home."

She passed car-lots, trailer courts, and small frame houses before the scene changed. Between pillars she drove into a leafy, somnolent neighborhood, peaceful, southern, and slightly antique. Lawns and leaves shared the same misty shade of midsummer-green, and willows abounded. The school was up a darkly shaded drive. Tennessee School.

For the Deaf. She'd found it in the phone book.

Summer was not the time to find children, but she came on a sort of pilgrimmage; a fool's errand.

What was she involving herself in? And why? She'd leave in a week for the marathon in North Carolina, surprise her folks on their fortieth anniversary in Indianapolis, and go check on a race near there before swinging south again to Kentucky. Always on the go. No reason to cultivate ties with the Strathgordons, or with Nicky. Never time. And, as the bard says, "so it goes."

She drove slowly around the loop drive, admiring shaded lush grass and trim brick buildings. This wasn't the oral school that Lanier had described; it was the state school for deaf children. So quiet, here. No open doors to walk into, no ears for her questions. Did this school hire "deaf-mute" teachers? Would Nicky be happy here? Would Nicky ever be happy, or whole?

"Brother! Am I ignorant!" she exclaimed.

Back in the heat of Knoxville, simmering in July, she treated herself to a matinee out on the Pike, lunching on Jordan almonds in the dark, chilly theater. The movie made her cry.

She didn't feel like going home to Sue's empty house, so she stopped by the University library under its magnolia trees, not a bit out of her way.

Its card-catalog featured multitudes of entries under "Deafness." Dozens of books did exist about making kids talk, listen, and lipread, but she didn't feel like requesting stack-privileges or studying books.

Outside, under a magnolia tree barely stirring its leaves, she sat down on a bench, sad to feel thwarted. She might telephone the Strathgordons and ask, "How's Nicky today?" Or, "Can I please take Nicky somewhere with me, give your child a breath of free air?"

Annalee dared not let him play outside, she said, for fear she couldn't catch up with him if he again tried to run away.

Why not take a run? Change clothes in the car, where she always kept extra shorts and T-shirt, and take the excellent jog-trail that began up by the highway crossing? But the car by now would be oppressively hot, a sauna. Better to jog at night. You won't get mugged in friendly, sleepy, upright "Knoxvul."

She strolled past students waiting for buses, and one prematurely gray youth—she'd seen several—smiled a good-ole-boy smile at her.

"Do you know anyone studying deaf-education?" she boldly asked.

He didn't. But he did have a beautiful smile.

Someone ought to. Someone must be able to tell her something, on a big University campus. She crossed the street to the Student Union.

Wandering around the air-conditioned halls, she set her mind to sorting out race-preparations for Pine Mountain. In her camper would arrive boxfuls of trophies and T-shirts, Dad's award-shirts with mountain laurel against a dark green background under white letters spelling out "Pine Mountain Marathon." Very pretty. Today's phone call reassured her that the portable toilets were soon expected to arrive (Pray God), and the ERG mix was there. Her team was buying brand-new plastic garbage cans to hold drinks for their runners. Ladies would soon fill brown envelopes with course-maps, home-made bib-numbers, and safety-pins.

The whole process dove-tailed when race-officials proved dependable, and these people were. Cautious and responsible and trustworthy, and worried sick that someone would die.

Marti read wall-posters, peered into the bookstore, and decided that southern college-girls come in only one variety—pretty. Or were they, too, now "college-women"? When she asked where people study about the handicapped, she was given the name "Philander Claxton Hall."

Cute. Classes weren't in session—it was the break between summer school terms, but secretaries toiled in lonely offices on the ground floor of Claxton. Most professors were out of town, but Marti obtained numbers for a teacher and two grad students, as well as for "a local businessman" who sometimes came in to interpret.

She phoned the students, first. They'd be closer to her age, and the label "businessman" called up an image of fat, balding, pushy lugs in polyester suits.

No one was home of the three. So she took herself back across the Pike and three blocks down Clinch to the restaurant the businessman owned. She was ready for dinner, if not for an interview with him.

The dinner was more than ample. Liver and onions, rice and apple cobbler in a cozy setting that fit its name: Wander Inn.

Marti looked around for hand-signs, but expected and glimpsed none. There was one harried waitress and a man who ran full plates out from the kitchen to be ferried to customers.

He wore a white apron, and was tan, tousled, and quick on his feet. Pouches under his eyes gave him a wistful, bloodhound look, and made his age tough to judge—twenty-five to forty. He had a nice square jaw. His jeans sagged down, almost covering his running shoes. So homely he was cute.

She was ready to leave when she noted that besides the running shoes—that everyone wears, nowadays—he had another sign of the runner. The faded jeans stretched tightly across his calves and thighs. A dead give-away. And he was far from plump.

"Do you run?" she asked, when he paused to back-hand perspiration off his brow.

"Doesn't everyone?" he responded in a soft drawl. And then he grinned, and she decided he wasn't nearly forty. Surely he knew the cafe owner. When he reached for her plate, she dropped her eyes and contemplated her own hand, its fingers and thumb almost inadvertently in the position Nicky showed her.

"You DO?" he exclaimed, grinning wider.

She mustn't have blushed in a year, but she did.

"You know sign language?" she stammered.

"Doesn't everyone? You lookin' for a class? They don't start up again til second term, but there's several at U.T."

"No, that's not . . . that's not for me," she said. "I would if you don't mind, if you get a break—I would like to ask a couple questions about a little boy."

He excused himself, unloaded the heavy crockery in the kitchen and returned, plopping down opposite her in the booth, arms on the table between them. "Go on. Ask me. Everybody else does."

Comedian. But he carried it off.

"Okay. I meant to ask . . . I need to know . . . how long does it take for a little deaf kid to talk?"

"To talk," he echoed, and wasn't grinning anymore.

"I mean, so people can understand him."

"How old is he? When was he deafened?" She told him. Nine; deaf at birth. "He wears hearing aids in both ears, but I don't think he hears anything much. He seems awfully frustrated. I don't know enough about it, and—"

"What's his name? Where does he live?"

"Are you the owner of this place?" she parried, intimidated by the way he leaned further and further forward as his fists knotted up.

"Partly. In partnership. Why?"

"You interpret at the University?"

"Sure. Deaf students do need to know what their professors say."

What was ailing him?

"I didn't introduce myself," she said. "Marti Hanson. I'm in town for a short while, I can't involve myself, but-"

"Joel Dalton." He stuck out a hand and she took it. Her hand came back to her scented with onions. "Now say that again. A born-deaf kid lives here, and at nine he's supposed to be learning to talk?"

"That's awfully late, isn't it? I was afraid that was the problem."

"How does he communicate?" the man said, eyes narrowing.

"Well, of course he has to be broken . . . discouraged from using his hands, so he'll talk more clearly, and the only way they know is to limit signs . . . and try to persuade. . . ."

His lips moved, brows drew down, but he didn't speak.

"You see, his mother ruined him. She started him out early with gestures and deaf-mute teachers, and now his divorced father and his step-mother are trying to–"

"Where do they live?"

"I might be able to bring him here to meet you," she murmured, not saying Nicky's name, "But I don't feel free to give out his address. Maybe you know what's holding him back? Maybe he's tongue-tied, or something?"

Joel said, "Why don't we get together when I close up this place at eight?"

He must have seen her edging away from him, toward the door.

"Give me your phone number, at least."

She told him her phone number, and when they both stood up, he wasn't much taller than she, maybe five-eight or nine. He looked very worried. Brown hair, brown tan, flat stomach. No more grin.

"Sorry I'm so rushed. It's dinner-time. But I'll sure call you. We've got to talk about this."

"Do we?" she asked herself on the sidewalk heading back to the car. "MUST we?"

She might prefer to talk to Joel about things less controversial than Nicky. Like running. Or the fate of a four-year-old marathoner at Pine Mountain. Hey, was Joel Dalton planning to run Pine Mountain? It was only a short, scenic drive. Or short by her standards. Why hadn't she asked him that?

The only thing wrong with Knoxville was the absence of friends, here.

Lonelytown, Tennessee.

Nicky

Nicky wanted his lady to come back. She wasn't wonderful, but she was the best he knew, and he was sick, sick of here.

He hated Daddy and the deaf man who was crazy, and even Fat-mother who cried a lot. He hated food, now, and bedtime, and the day it rained so he couldn't even lean out the window. He started breaking things to make them mad, when he wasn't crying like blind, and he threw up his dinner a lot. Maybe they'd call a doctor like his doctor at home, or Grandma would come. He didn't know what day or month or week it was, because he didn't know what day he came, and didn't have any way to mark off days, like they do in jail on the wall. How long would he stay?

It might be forever.

They talked on the phone a lot, jumping up to show it rang, but never telling him—even writing it—who called. Did Grandma and Grandpa Katz call, or Kirby or his sisters? Did they know he'd come here from Lexington and wanted so bad to go back? Go anywhere.

When his stomach hurt in the night, he couldn't tell them, because he couldn't get out of his room, and no one came, anymore, when he pounded. He guessed he pounded too much, like all night once. Elyse said that was like crying, "Wolf,

wolf, wolf!" but she didn't say why. Dogs say "Wolf, wolf."

Daddy got older and older-looking, and Nicky saw him yelling at Step-mother. Nobody tied his hands, anymore, but they put him into the little desk he'd peed into. To talk. The bad man came every day when the clock said four-thirty, but he didn't slap anymore. Daddy shook his head no.

Now he knew fat lady was step-mother, he tried calling her by name, and once she understood and hugged him harder than ever. "Step" was hard, but he did "mother" right. He tried to tell her fat stomachs come from cookies and candy, and go away with tennis. He mimed playing tennis with an invisible racket; he threw the ball up high and served it, but she didn't catch on until he ran back and forth across the livingroom hitting the ball, backhand, fronthand. Then she laughed and pointed at him and hugged him again.

This perfume smelt better than before. Like sweet peas. She put stuff on her face. Mama didn't. Wicked Mama that didn't write to him.

"Play tennis and you won't grow fat stomach," he told Step-mother, pointing at her. He patted her tummy and shook his head. Then he remembered. Fat-stomach means baby. He rocked a baby in his arms—the sign for "baby," and made question-face, and patted her tummy, and she got smart and understood. She shook head no, and laughed, and then looked sad.

He said, "You want baby?" and then said it three times more, and her mouth said, "Your Daddy . . ." and her head shook no. Daddy doesn't want baby.

He was sorry and glad. Daddy had four children already. But if Daddy had baby, he might let Nicky go.

His Love-lady was best, but still, she was scared of Daddy.

"Speak with voice," she had said, pointing to her mouth, and holding both his hands in one of hers. "Daddy" (he could read that when she pointed behind her toward the door) "wants you" (pointing at him) "to talk . . ." Something. Something again. But he'd TRIED! He'd talked and talked in school, til the teachers said he wasn't a talking kind of kid. Mrs. Elliott used to make a game: his mouth was a dark cave, and his teeth were pearls, and his tongue was a big fish that lived in the cave and darted out, and then lay down to sleep. That's when he was very little. When he made a word well, she'd hug him, and when he didn't, she breathed a big breath and asked him real nice to try again, try again. Then she gave him big boy's books to read and signed, "You read wonderfully."

That had pleased him. Mama read to him since he could remember, and he learned to fingerspell words on his hand before he could read. That made it easy to read alone when he was five. He read "grade-level," which was fourth. He just couldn't control his voice. It came out all wrong. Hearies said "talk, talk," but when he did, they made faces as if his mouth made a bad fart, and anyway, deaf friends who could talk were always getting banana ice cream when they asked for vanilla.

He wanted Love-lady to come back. He remembered she let signs come on TV and let him write, and he had a zillion things to ask her. When she was here, he wanted to get her name and address. It made him ache, wanting to know so badly. He had touched her arm, and she looked around and smiled like love at him, so he filled his lungs the way they taught him to blow out candles, and said, "What is your name?"

"What?" she said, holding a cup and a plate.

"Your address?" The "O" of "your" was surely right, and the "A" of "name," but "address" was never clear on the lips. Most words looked like chewing, anyhow. He made writing motions.

"No. Writing is bad," she said, shaking her head.

He kicked the sink. Not her, just the sink. If he ever kicked Love-lady, he wouldn't have anybody.

Suddenly, Step-mother made listen-face and got up and ran to the door. Nicky ran after her. At the door there was Love-lady in an orange dress. A little car stood in the driveway, not her camper-truck. He didn't dare make a sign, but he pulled her quickly inside, wondering if Step-Mother would go away and let them talk. He had so much to say, and it was almost time for bad deaf man.

Love-lady had kisses, and looked at him different, with part of her mouth aiming up and part aiming down, like smile-frown. Step-mother went away. He was very glad. Four o'clock. Daddy came home at six. Deaf man must not come. Love-lady said something very carefully, and held onto his shoulders and made him look at her. (She never pinched his face in her hand to make him look.) He didn't get any words. Maybe one was "want." "I want." What did she want, with sad face and worried? Worried eyes. "I take"? I take you . . .
. . .where?

He turned on the TV, and she turned it right off. He picked up her purse, and she took it away. He knew he was in trouble. Where did she want to take him? He wanted to go with her. Anywhere.

Then she made the same listen-face, but didn't go to the telephone and pick it up. She went to the door.

Nicky saw who it was, and he ran down the hall, away, and into his room, and slammed the door hard as he could, and began to cry. He got down and crawled under his bed and rolled up very small.

And wiped his nose. And waited.

Marti

The man who stood under the Strathgordons' portico was so tall, clean-cut and fresh-faced that she would have called him a Mormon missionary if she hadn't suspected Annalee had something like this up her sleeve. Babysit at four o'clock on Friday, when Lanier was at work and Annalee just must go see the insurance man? Insurance for what? To pay for all the valuables Nicky was breaking?

She wasn't quite sure though, until his first words gave her the answer.

He dipped his head—a boyish cow-lick falling forward—smiled, and said, "Me Manny Ahnsah?"

Miss Marti Hanson? She recognized her own name on his non-mute tongue.

Marti invited him in, in his neat brown suit, striped tie and polished shoes. There was no one in town she was more eager to meet.

"I presume you're Mr. Teague?" she asked, forgot to face him when she said it, and had to repeat, just as he said, "Ah ham Alan Teague."

He did a splendid job with his name. Lots of practice.

The famous deaf man who talked! Yes, he was attractive, his costume color-coordinated and expensive, eyes bright and alert. There was no sign of his defect beyond the effort he put into speaking and the less-than-perfect result. She wasn't to babysit alone, then? She was to sit them both, Nicky and Alan?

"Call me Alan," he smiled, put out his hand, shook hers, and didn't let go. Oh boy. Chemistry. How long to get used to his voice? Bigot! Compare his speech with Nicky's, and forgive the lack of inflection and resonance. And the pronunciation. Pretend he's a Turk or a Finn, in spite of that all-American face.

"Let us talk about Nicky," she said carefully and slowly. And softly. Volume was no factor. He didn't even wear a hearing aid. He must have caught the last words, for he said, "Yes, we all must cooperate to save Nicky."

"Will I see you give him a lesson?" she asked without enthusiasm. The fleeing child and slamming door left the house silent. She'd listened for shattering glass that would mean Nicky had dived headfirst out the window, but silence prevailed.

"Lessons are difficult," Alan said. "I was forced to take extreme measures once with Nicky. To restrain him. I haven't been able to sleep since, remembering—" He shook his head miserably. "May I make myself a drink? I leave work early, to help Nicky. My position is with the Tennessee Valley Authority, TVA. If I arrive at eight o'clock in the morning, I may leave at four to come here. Will you have a drink with me?" That's what she figured he said.

She was not a cocktail-hour person; she preferred to earn an occasional beer with a long, hot run, but she let the man make use of the Strathgordon bar to prepare her a Margarita.

She'd asked for a Manhattan.

While he downed his Martini and made himself a second one, smiling a bit apologetically, she studied his silver cufflinks, reddish hair, nicely styled, and strong nose. Joel Dalton was cute; Alan was handsome, and she could understand almost everything he said. Divorced? Fortyish. He was once just like Nicky? Wow.

"You can't be totally deaf," she said, as an opener, once he was seated on the couch and indicated she should sit beside him, turned to face him.

"Ahm so deaf, ah oos no eeing aye." He turned his head to right and to left to show her. "Nanny debells."

"Huh?"

He said it again, and she understood. No hearing aids. Ninety decibels' loss. "Same as Nicky. We wan Nicky to be like me."

"I should think so!"

"Beg pardon?"

"Yes." Nodding. "I agree. That would be won-der-ful."

"You shall help me," he said, and patted her hand. "Nickee does na know whateh is good for him."

She found that by watching his lips she understood him much better.

"Where is Nicky?" he asked.

"He ran away."

"Yes, I heard that he ran away. You found him. For that his father will be forever grateful. You saved his body, and we now must save his mind."

"Tell me about yourself," she said.

Alan put down his empty glass; he did not eat the olive, and she watched him shake his head thoughtfully. "Ma mother worked very hard, teaching me. All the time. She never let me sign. Only deaf-mutes sign, not me. I do not associate with deaf."

"Do not what?"

"A-ssociate. Socialize with deaf people. They lead very limited lives. Their horizons are extremely narrow, and many cannot read or write. I have never met deaf people. My friends all are hearing."

"You're divorced?"

"My wife was hearing. We came to a parting of the ways. No matter."

"Children?"

"Fortunately, none. No. So you see why I love Nicky. He is, in a sense, like my own little boy."

He kept staring at her naked ring-finger.

"I'll call Nicky," she said, then remembered. "Shall I go get Nicky?"

Alan gave a great sigh. "I hate to have you exposed to the . . .the conflicts that arise. We are not uptight with each other."

Huh? Then she caught on. He took "uptight" to mean congenial.

"In fact," he went on, "I would prefer not to give a lesson today. When Mr. and Mrs. Strathgordon return, why do you not go to dinner with me, and we shall attend a Discotheque? Do you like dancing?"

She said, "I adore dancing," before it hit her. A deaf man? DANCING? What was this, a segment of some show like "That's Incredible"?

"Did you say dancing?" she asked him.

"Yes, dancing. Do I surprise you?" A glowing smile. He had blue eyes. "Yes, I dance."

She'd worn a dress today, for once, a cool, flowered wraparound that would be perfect, and strappy sandals without much heel. Hey, this was very sudden, but it was Friday, and she hadn't had a date for a month. What did he drive? DID he drive?

She told herself to come back down to earth. She was Nicky's sitter. She couldn't leave unless his parents returned, and where was Nicky? How was he? Jumping up, she motioned for Alan to stay put, and went down the hall to Nicky's room.

Nicky wasn't there. In a panic, she looked around her. She would have heard the door open, and the window still was nailed shut.

"Nickeeee?" she wailed.

No answer.

Then she bent over and listened very hard. Very clearly she now heard breathing.

Breathing? Were her ears that good to make up for nearsightedness? Yes, there was someone in this room breathing. Under the bed.

She knelt down, lifted the skirts of the bedspread, and there were two eyes.

"Nicky, come out. He won't hurt you," she said. Motioned "come," shook her head "won't hurt," and smiled. Nicky shook his head no. She half lay down and reached for him, got a piece of arm, and tugged. He moaned. She pulled harder. Good old race-training; it builds up arm-strength, too. She retrieved Nicky, kissed him, dried his wet face on the edge of the bedsheet, smoothed down his hair, and led him by the hand out of his room.

When he saw Alan, the child burst into a windmill of hitting and kicking, taking her by surprise. Alan leaped to her aid, and was tumbled over backwards, sitting down very hard and striking his elbow on the coffee-table.

"I cannot teach this child!" he cried in exasperation.

Marti had to sit on the couch with Nicky curled across her-lap, hiding his head behind her, ostrich-fashion.

"Oh, my," she panted, stroking the boy.

And that was the moment for Nicky's parents to unlock the front door and come in. Nicky didn't know it.

"How are you two getting along?" asked Annalee brightly. "Oh, oh! Nicky's being bad again, isn't he?"

"So what else is new?" snapped his father. "I'm sorry, Alan. No lesson, today?"

Alan looked up at him, and Lanier repeated the question, getting the affirmative he expected.

"Well, we'll take over," said Annalee. "Why don't you and Marti take a little drive? Show her Knoxville, Alan. She's new here."

It was done. Marti pried Nicky loose, gave him to his father, and nodded to Alan Teague. Break-time. Consultation. Dinner out, Disco, and then another assault could be launched upon Nicky's stubborn resistance. No wonder Lanier wanted Nicky to grow up like Alan . . . and Annalee wanted her to meet Nicky's teacher.

Alan took Marti's arm to lead her down the walk to the driveway where he'd parked behind her. The Strathgordon's car was blocking hers, but not blocking his Camaro. She stowed all conversation until the first stoplight. Nervous with him driving, she relaxed when she realized that his busy eyes were watching the road, the rearview mirror and both outside mirrors, all the time. He didn't even need glasses. He smelled of some expensive after-shave. British Sterling? Or English Leather? When had he time to shave after work?

"Mr. Strathgordon was like my father. He left home, too. But my mother was better than Nicky's, not lazy and uncaring. Nicky was treated like a puppy-dog, not a real person. You can gesture to animals; you must talk, talk, talk, to a deaf child."

"I see." She was straining to comprehend his voice.

He took her to dinner at Regas restaurant, but in the dark and elegant interior she had trouble making her lips clear. So Alan talked, talked about his interesting job with computers, described his and Mr. Strathgordon's similar mathematical backgrounds. "My salary," he said, "is twenty-one thousand dollars a year."

"That is very good," she said, nodding emphatically over her prime rib.

"Do you know what deaf people earn who peddle alphabet cards?"

"I can imagine."

"They are exploited, too. It is disgraceful."

Then he told her she looked "lovey" (lovely), and called her "Manny" one time too many. She took out her pen and wrote on the edge of her napkin, "Marti. Short for Martha."

"Oh, I see!" he cried, embarassed. "Names prove difficult." He asked her to write "Hanson" for him, too, and her address. (Phone number? No, stupid. He'd have to have someone phone for him, wouldn't he?)

"How do you dance?" she asked. No way could she have held back that question any longer.

"I feel the sound on my face. The floor vibrates. And there are other dancers to serve as my examples" (aye-amuls).

"Aren't you really just hard of hearing? Can you use a telephone?"

She put her fist near her face as if holding a receiver.

"No, No phone. Not even with an amplifier. I have never heard a sound, Manti."

The Disco was so ear-blasting that she found it impossible to understand his mechanical monotone–robot-voice. The music might deafen her, too, make her a perfect match for him. Darkness to prevent lipreading, noise to prevent hearing, so all the other patrons were shouting at each other. But the music began to excite her, to coincide with her heartbeat, and dancing was fun. He was good at it, his senses of timing and rhythm excellent. Running had lent her the stamina to dance all night, but she didn't wear him out. She tried to communicate in body-English that she didn't desire hugs or stolen kisses when they sat out a dance, wondering whom he dated, since he stressed over and over that he never associated with "deaf-mutes."

She began to practice in advance the phrases she wanted to use, checking for visibility. An interesting exercise in linguistics, but it put a damper on conversation. She wondered if Nicky could lipread Alan, and how Alan could hear Nicky's speech—such as it was.

She took out her pen and again wrote on the cocktail napkin. "How long til Nicky talks like you?"

He frowned and shrugged. "All are different," he wrote. "Who can tell?"

Too much of a challenge to get across to him what SHE did for a living, for a net $6,000 last year, so she didn't try. Her pet ice-breaking line, "I've never run more than thirteen miles, but my job is running marathons," would not compute, even if he knew the distance and the pun.

Better to dance, to twirl around Alan, arch her back over his wrist and swing her hips as he did. What a tireless partner. She could be thankful at least for that. He was something to write home about . . . or to Ripley's "Believe it or not."

She'd left her car at the Strathgordon's, so he drove her there around midnight; she was watching the road intently for him as if he were blind. Funny how she got confused. Should she take his arm and lead him, whisper to him what was going on? Even after spending hours with Nicky and Alan, it was easier to think of them as blind. She'd never met one deaf person Nicky's age, or Alan's, either.

He had a bit too much to drink, and she'd have preferred to drive, but that might insult him. "Hire the Handicapped," said posters. How about "Date the Handicapped"? She'd been out with a one-eyed man once, and lots of times with injured runners who had to lean heavily on her and groan, but this?

Outside his car in the Strathgordon driveway, he kissed her, and her hands rose without bidding to touch his ears.

"Ooo don need ease to may lave," he said.

No you don't need ears to make love, only to listen with. Hands were for talking. No, hands were for touching, for love-making. She didn't have all her questions answered. She'd had a good time, but . . . but . . . Great guy, great triumph. Salary four times hers. Divorced–why and when? How did he teach Nicky? Suddenly she remembered Lanier saying that always one of them was there, he or Annalee, to check Nicky's pronunciation.

Why did Nicky chop the hands off his doll? She'd for awhile wondered if his teacher did it as an object-lesson, but after tonight, she knew Alan wasn't the type. He was a pussycat.

There seemed to be some factor missing from the equation. Good mothers turn out Alan Teagues; bad mothers turn out Nicky Strathgordons, called deaf-mutes. But why hadn't she met a few Alans, before this thirtieth year of her life? She had more friends than she could count, spread all over kingdom-come. And her friends had friends. Never in her life had she even heard of a phenomenon like Alan, much less talked with one. Yet more and more you saw sign-language on TV and even on the street; there were stories about it in the newspaper. Old people went deaf like her grandparents who said, "Eh, speak up, Marti," and cupped hand behind ear, but that wasn't the same. They could talk. She shook her head, dizzy and very tired. Nicky, strong drink, much dancing, and their communication difficulties made it a long, long evening.

Alan and Marti walked into the house to find Lanier and Annalee sitting collapsed in the livingroom.

"What happened to you?" Marti demanded.

"Nicky was taking a bath and never turned off the water," his father reported. "Completely flooded the bathroom. It's a good thing there seems to be a slope to the house, so it ran into the laundry room and out the back porch. It's just too much."

"Lanier is tempted to send Nicky back to his grandparents in Kentucky," Annalee said. "But I think that's giving in too early. There's two weeks left, and they don't know we have troubles with Nicky. We tell them everything's fine, and I think we ought to just persevere, don't you?"

"Will you please repeat?" said Alan.

When the repetition was finished, so Alan saw what the rest of them heard, Marti got up from her chair shaking her head. "Beats me! Lanier, do you know a man named Joel Dalton?"

"No, I don't."

"He's a sign-language interpreter. I just wondered."

"That is one thing we do NOT need," he said. "Nicky's had enough of those to last a lifetime. Or, to put it more accurately, to wreck his life. Don't you want him to be like Alan, now you've gotten to know Alan?"

"You both look so darling," Annalee said, brightening. "I bet you had a wonderful time. He tells us how good a dancer he is. Isn't he? If I weren't a married lady, I'd like to go out dancing with Alan," she teased, nudging her husband.

"Yes?" Alan said, inclining his head toward Annalee.

Marti punched him lightly, got his attention, and said, "Yes, Alan dances very well" (emphatically). "I had a good time. Thank you for suggesting it."

"There's a Kiwanis dinner tomorrow night," said Annalee. "I don't suppose--"

"You want me to sit again?" Marti exclaimed, but she hadn't kept Nicky very long today. Only from four to five. "Sure. What time?"

Alan was at the bar. No wonder. With three of them talking, he found it hard to catch everything. She wondered if tomorrow was a set-up, too, and Alan would reappear to keep her company. That left her with very mixed feelings, but it would be awkward to say anything.

"Seven p.m.," said Annalee.

"I'll have to move my car to let you out," said Lanier. "Sorry. I was about to do that, when Nicky distracted us." He got out his key-ring, and Marti went right along with him, after touching Alan's elbow, nodding, smiling, and thanking him for the swell evening. Alan started to follow her, looked at his full glass, and she said, "That's okay. See you again, sometime."

The car moved, goodbyes said, she backed the Mazda, turned, put it into neutral, and let it roll down the driveway to the county road, glad to be going home alone, and wondering why she agreed to sit again tomorrow night.

She felt sorry Alan had her address. She also felt confused and sad. She ought to have gone in to see Nicky. Little demon. Flooded the bathroom, this time, had he? Why? Didn't he see the advantages of being an Alan Teague? Didn't he wish he had a mother like Alan's? Would Nicky ever be able to dance at a Disco, on a date with a hearing woman?

What woke her at seven a.m. was the telephone by the bed. She cuddled under the covers with the receiver, so the voice rose out of the dark right into her ear. A great advantage of living sometimes in a house—talking on the phone from bed, cozy and warm. Alan could never do that; never had, poor guy.

It was not Alan on the phone. It was Joel Dalton.

"I thought you might come over with the kid the last couple of days. I've been calling you and calling. You're impossible to get hold of."

"I've been out a lot. I sat with him last night, and will tonight–" she'd said too much, too fast.

"You sit him tonight, too?"

"I didn't mean–Look, I'll see if I can get permission to take him to town to meet you."

"He doesn't live in town?"

"Joel, don't be so persistent! It's really a mess, out there. The kid is destructive, and the people are so nice. Stymied."

"Let me come out to look at the kid. Marti, this could be very, very bad for him. For a deaf kid. Does he cry a lot? Are you absolutely forbidden to use any signs?"

"I don't know any signs. Just that one . . . I showed you," she said lamely. "They know a born-deaf man who talks well, and he's Nicky's role-model. I'm not sure I can leave the house with Nicky. He ran away, once, so they're scared."

"Ran away? Was it reported?"

"I found him. That's how I got mixed up in all this."

"Were the police involved?"

"Yeah. But that's irrelevant. They watch him very closely now. Look, just tell me where I can reach you, and I'll phone from their house."

"I'll be at work. It's in the book. You won't say where the house is, then? You're that stubborn?"

"Yes, I am. Mr. . . . his father says an interpreter is what they do NOT need. I asked if he knew you, but he didn't."

Joel grunted. Marti rolled up in a tighter ball under the covers, like Nicky under his bed. At seven, where was Joel; in bed, too? She asked him.

"No, I bake. I'm at work. Home-made bread for breakfast has to be baked damned early in the morning."

"Sounds delicious."

"Tell me where YOU live, and I'll bring you over some, right after breakfast; I'm off for two hours."

She was very much tempted, but she put him off. Joel was in a sense their enemy, not a friend, and a cute runner who came walking into this lonely house carrying hot, fresh-baked bread, with her still in a nightie, drowsy– nope. Dream-material, not wise at all. Be fun to throw Joel together with Alan, though, and see what transpired. Pistols at twenty paces? Back to back, ready-go; halt, turn and fire?

The trouble was, she told herself as she said goodbye to Joel, she wasn't sure which man she'd root for.

When Marti reached the Strathgordon house at seven, Nicky came running and clung to her waist, sobbing so she crouched down to hug him, glaring up at his father, who poured out his fears to her.

"Nicky, I'm beginning to think, is retarded. You can't judge by how he does at school; they can't have any standards. Maybe minimally brain-damaged? We're at our wits' end. He says 'No,' and a few other words very clearly, but he acts as if he hates us. Poor Annalee tries so hard, she bribes him with sweets, but now he won't eat anything. No supper last night; no breakfast, lunch, or dinner today." He threw up his hands. "I've got to run upstairs and finish dressing. We're late."

She was left holding the boy. Lanier was no sooner out of sight than someone came through the open front door right behind her.

Nicky

The man's eyes, over Love-Lady's shoulder, looked at Nicky so hard Nicky couldn't breathe.

She put him down, turned around, and made fast-mouth, but the man leaned over and touched him. Nicky didn't get either hand up before the man signed, "You Nickie?"

A stab went through him like a knife. His eyes shot out of his face like rockets. First time, forever and ever, a person was talking to him!

His name was spelled wrong, but the man knew his name, and then he said, "You deaf?"

Nicky opened wide arms and grabbed onto him, hugging, and had to rear back, wiping eyes, to see words, words, words, like milk and honey and candy and fresh air and sun all coming off his fingers, falling on Nicky, coming close to his face–beautiful, fast, clear words Nicky understood.

"Deaf, me not. Hearing, me," the man signed, and then, "Deaf, mother and father. Help you, me?" Man didn't talk.

Nicky signed, "Understand! Take me home. I want Pittsburgh!"

The man stopped down and picked him up and patted his back. When Love-lady came close, with dumb hands, reaching for him, Nicky kicked at her, and the man spun round so she couldn't get him or get kicked.

Nicky had to talk, fast, fast, but he was crying. Ashamed, afraid he'd lose the wonderful, wonderful man, he let go enough to be able to sign, "I die here. Take me away!" He said "Pittsburgh" real well and signed it on his chest.

The man nodded. He made big eyes, and so did Love-lady. Who sent the man, and did it mean he was safe?

The man sat down on the couch and stood Nicky between his knees, holding him up; when he had hands free, the man said, "Me, Joel Dalton," and asked what Nicky was feeling.

Nicky told him. And told him. Everything, so he said "Slower," and Nicky told him again.

"Quiet, quiet; I won't leave you," Joel Dalton said. "Don't cry."

Love-lady was saying things with mouth, flutter-flutter, so Nicky asked, "Who is she? What she say?"

"You don't know her name?" he asked, so Nicky felt ashamed when he read the name "Marti Hanson" spelled twice on Joel's fast fingers. He memorized it.

"Interpret her," he demanded.

Nicky still had tears tickling his face, but couldn't help being a baby. He wanted words, flying fast, so fast. He got an arm around Joel, and climbed on his knee, and Joel's hands signed right under their noses, while Marti Hanson twisted dumb hands, her mouth saying what Joel signed for her: "Afraid! His father will KILL you!"

Nicky hoped Joel would kill Daddy right back.

"How did you find this house?" (Joel signed that Marti said.)

"I know police. All my friends. I interpret for them; they told me."

Joel signed with sharp, angry, short signs, his mouth turning down. He said Daddy was "misled," and turned to Marti and kept right on signing when he talked to her. She asked why, and he said, "For Nicky."

She said, "Oh," with open mouth and surprise-eyes.

Nicky told Joel about crazy man tying him to the desk, and Joel got madder. Joel asked did Marti know about tying, and she said yes, and Joel said why didn't she call the cops. Then her mouth turned down, and Nicky watched tears shine out of her eyes.

Nicky asked how did Joel know so much, and he said, "I was born signing."

That must look funny, a little new baby signing, and Nicky wondered if Joel made his first sign when the nurse wrapped him up in a blanket, or if he was signing when he first came out of his mama's sitting-down place.

Now Marti ran upstairs. Nicky talked and talked to Joel, saying things he'd wanted or hated for a long, long time. If he needed toilet, Joel would know, and if he didn't like asparagus, and if he missed his white cat at home who was deaf, too. Joel signed faster than Mama. He would never let Joel go away and leave him.

But Joel didn't say he'd take Nicky to Pittsburgh.

When Marti came back, she said, "I feel so stupid," so Joel taught her to hit her head and point to herself, which means, "I am stupid." Nicky was so glad to see her getting smart that he threw her a kiss, like hearies do. Smarti Marti. When Joel made her rub her fist on her chest for "Sorry," he did kiss her. She held him and kissed him on the hair, and then she made the "I-love-you" sign that Nicky taught her first of all.

"Take me to Lexington," said Nicky to Joel, but Joel frowned. "Put me on the bus to Pittsburgh, then.

"On the bus to Lexington?" he asked. "Please?"

Then Marti's head shot up, but Nicky was the first one to see Daddy coming down the stairs. He jumped toward Joel as fast as he could and held onto him tight. He didn't look up.

Marti

Joel Dalton rose to his feet abruptly, lifting Nicky with him, and his face grew lined with strain. Short and lightly built as he was, he looked capable of throwing a punch. If only it were not Daddy, but Alan, coming into the room. Alan was the person Joel needed to meet, to see what could be possible for Nicky's future.

"Watch him start something," Joel muttered, and she didn't like the tone of his voice; Nicky's expression was absolutely wretched.

"That is my son," Lanier said.

Annalee was on the stairs, hastening to catch up with him, fastening an earring.

Nicky fastened himself to Joel like a monkey on a pole, arms and legs wound around him.

No act of aggression—verbal or physical—would have been more provocative than Joel's signing as he said, "I'm Joel Dalton. I'm very much concerned about your son."

"What are you doing?" the older man cried.

"Because there's a deaf person here, I'm signing. Why not?"

Nicky did not look up. He had his face pushed into Joel's chest.

Marti said, "Let me explain. I met Joel this Wednesday through the Special Education Department—Joel's an interpreter, and—"

"I don't need an interpreter for my own son!"

"Oh, yes you DO!" Joel snapped.

"You put him down this instant!"

"Shall I make us coffee?" Annalee offered. "Let's all sit down, and—"

"I can't put him down. I'm not holding him."

Joel opened his arms straight out to the sides, but Nicky remained where he hung. Lanier took two steps toward Joel and gripped Nicky around the waist. He jerked. Nicky howled appallingly. Joel continued to stand there almost nonchalantly, stretching out his arms, staring into the older, bigger man's face.

Marti could hardly bear it.

Of course, Nicky's small strength was soon overcome. He was torn loose from Joel, and began fighting his father, who lost his grip on him, but blocked him off from Joel. Nicky, sobbing, tore down the hall out of sight.

"I've just today baked a nice sponge cake. Would you like coffee and cake, Joel? Or shall we each have a cup of tea?"

No one listened.

"How could you let this man into my house?" Lanier turned to Marti.

"She didn't let me in. I forced my way in. She refused to say where you lived, so I got it from another source. Don't blame her. You'd better send Nicky back to his mother, or I may talk to some good friends of mine down at the police station."

Lanier Strathgordon wasn't pale anymore. Streaks of red flew up his neck and cheeks; even his ears darkened.

"Joel can tell you what Nicky says, and let Nicky know what each of us says," Marti pleaded. "There's so much to Nicky—"

"I want to hear my own son, for myself," Lanier cried, his voice almost breaking. "I refuse to depend on a crutch—another person, or hand-language. Damn it to hell, I want my son to be NORMAL!"

"Better worry about him being alive," Joel said very softly, giving Marti chills. "He's dying, and you're killing him."

"How dare you say that!"

"Listen to Joel. Please listen to Joel!" Marti put her hand on Lanier Strathgordon's arm, but he shook it off.

"Please don't fight," said Annalee, but only Marti heard her.

"I have sacrificed," Lanier said. "I camped out, alone, for six years, and sent all my money to Nicky. Would you do that, after a divorce? I'd give him anything!"

"Very defensive," Joel murmured.

"What right have you—?"

"A birth-right," Joel said. "My parents are deaf."

"Get out of my house."

"What?" Joel said.

"I said get out of my house!"

Nicky was peering around the corner, and Marti watched Annalee tiptoe over to him and get a grip on the child's hand. She herself could not move a finger.

"You think YOU're gonna be able to handle Nicky after he's been able to talk with me?" Joel said scathingly. "Do you? Just TRY!"

And then Joel began rather theatrically backing toward the door, one step at a time.

Nicky became very oral, screaming "-OL! -OL! -OL!"

Joel did not sign to the child. Furiously glaring at Lanier Strathgordon, he turned on his heel–on his flare-heeled racing shoe–and exited.

Nicky went mad. He flung himself forward so Annalee lost her grip on him, and his father had to catch him. Nicky pummelled him with fists, screaming and screaming for Joel.

Marti could not look.

"Maybe he was right," Annalee was murmuring in a stricken, soft voice, making her husband's flaming face convulse.

Marti hadn't in years seen a middle-aged man cry, and she had to turn her face away.

"Where're his pills?" Lanier muttered. "He needs something . . . for his feelings."

"I don't believe in drugs for little children," Annalee responded, and Marti found her voice to second that. It was Annalee who took Nicky from his father's arms to carry him down the hall, Marti tagging after. They undressed him and put him to bed while he lay leaden, like a staring corpse.

"Something is awfully wrong, here," Marti told the woman. "Joel was terribly rude, but this is dangerous, psychologically. Maybe Nicky has mental problems, but something has to be done."

Annalee nodded, closing Nicky's door to a crack.

"His father does adore him. Honestly. He loves him more than he does me. You know how men are about sons; I don't blame him. He'd give up anything for Nicky. He just doesn't know what to give up next."

Annalee retreated into the bathroom to repair her face, and Marti found Lanier in the livingroom, deep in a chair, sitting bent forward, elbows on knees and hands dangling. No drink was in sight, and she wished he'd have one.

"He won't be a cute little boy forever," he said.

There was no denying that.

"What else can I do?" he asked. "Alan suffered the same way when he was little. Look at him, now! Alan and Nicky aren't . . . they don't even belong to the same SPECIES!"

Marti wandered from window to window, looking out at nothing. Was Joel gone, or was he sitting in a car watching the house? Suppose Alan's sainted mother had weakened, had doubted as she herself did, and allowed someone like Joel to befriend her son? He might be a deaf-mute, today.

"I suppose you're not to blame for his coming, but, God help us, Marti, don't spill all our troubles to people!"

She said nothing. After a few minutes, he looked up at her, and caught hold of her arm.

"Marti," he said. "Marti, what in God's name would YOU do?"

Nicky

Nicky woke up suddenly, aching. He stared at the strip of light across his ceiling, wondering why he felt so miserable. Then he woke up more and remembered. He'd talked to somebody and somebody talked to him, and answered his questions, and then Daddy made him leave. Joel would never come back again. Marti didn't talk. Daddy drove Joel away, and tomorrow when he woke up, Marti would be gone, too, and deaf man would come back, and tie him up. Nicky wanted to die.

He'd never see Joel again, the beautiful, wonderful man with words on his hands, who said so much and understood every thought Nicky had for all this long, awful time.

He slid out of bed, remembering that hearies could hear him, though he couldn't hear himself walk. He went to the door and saw Step-mother go past. So he pushed the door very, very slowly, wondering how that sounded. Water falling makes sound, but shadows don't; leaves make a sound, and the wind does, but the sun rises and sets silently, they said. Mama said.

But Mama didn't come save him like Joel tried to, and if she was dead, he wanted to be dead with her.

If she wasn't dead, he hated her for letting him hurt so much, so long. He'd make her cry and wish she never got married. He swallowed big lumps of crying down.

Daddy would feel very sorry if Nicky died. Also Stepmother.

He pushed the door til wood touched wood, because that makes noise. And doorknobs do. They make heads come around. It wasn't fair that ears can hear through doors and down halls any noise he made.

"I can't talk well. I ought to die," he admitted to himself for the first time.

He walked across the dark room to the window that was nailed shut. He pulled a chair to the window, very slowly and carefully, before he got fuzzy-eyed with tears and too scared to do it. He climbed on the chair and caught hold of the cord from the big curtains. He held it in two hands. His brother Kirby taught him knots, even in the dark.

He made a good, big knot.

Then he stood on the chair, biting his lip, frowning, and feeling very sorry for himself and furious at Mama and Daddy both, and at Marti for not running away with him, and at Joel, too, for letting Daddy drive him off. They all made him do this bad thing.

His hands suddenly stung like when the hairbrush hit them, and if anyone ever again came at him with handkerchiefs to tie him to a chair, he'd– He'd rather be dead.

So Nicky Strathgordon put the loop of cord over his head, with the big knot beside his ear, tightened it up, and counted to ten, his next birthday.

And then he jumped.

Marti

Annalee rescued her from Lanier's unanswerable question. She called Marti into the kitchen. "Help fix us a glass of wine and a piece of cake. Food always makes people feel better."

Marti's chore was to cut the angel food cake, but the cake sagged under her knife, giving no resistance. What was the trick? Heat the knife, or chill it? She shook her head, irked by the absurdity of dessert when nobody except Annalee wanted food. Lanier looked like a man about to throw up, green-tinged with despair.

He was at least mobile now. She heard a soft bumping noise down the hall, paused to listen, and then resumed sawing on the fleshy cake. Surgeon. What had Lanier said, the first night she was here? They were like surgeons, he and Annalee. Nicky, unfortunately, got no anesthesia.

Annalee stood in the kitchen arranging delicate stemmed goblets of port on yellow doilies on a silver tray. Marti heard her humming softly, in spite of the chaos of the evening that left Marti shaking.

"She's the Martha, in the kitchen," thought Marti, "solving problems with food, while I'm Mary in the midst of battle." That left Jesus and Lazarus. Which was Lanier, and which, Joel?

To make conversation, she said, "I'll miss Knoxville. I hit the road four days from now, when my cousin gets back from New York."

"What's your opinion of that sign-language man?" Annalee asked. "He didn't dress very nicely. Why did Nicky like him so?"

"LIKE him? Nicky adored him. Nicky didn't even know my name. He also wanted to know where his Daddy went every day. He had so many questions."

"Well, you'll have to talk to Lanier about it," she said, and carried the tray into the livingroom where Lanier still sat, chin on his fist, staring at nothing.

"Have a little pick-me-up, honey," said Annalee.

Lanier gulped his wine, pushed away the cake, and stood up. "We have to go, Marti. I'm one of the after-dinner speakers. I can't be absent."

"Can you also get along without me?" Annalee asked her. "I so want to hear his speech at the Club."

"Of course. You both run along. You'll be late; it's past eight, now."

"Happy hour's still going on," Annalee said. "I hope we won't make too much of a scene coming in. Is my dress all right, honey? I hurried, and then that man–" she turned around, smoothing the silken pleats over her hips. Lanier grunted.

"Don't let anyone in the house, understand? Go check on my son."

Then, suddenly, they were out the door. Marti watched from a window, seeing that no vehicle but hers, with her dog in it, was left in the driveway. If Joel was much of a distance-runner he might have come on foot. She shivered. If he came back again, and rang the doorbell, she'd suffer agonies of indecision about admitting him.

But Nicky was asleep, now; it wouldn't be wise to awaken him for any reason, even for Joel. Nicky. Right! She'd better run check on him, as Lanier asked. Poor, tormented, torn-up Lanier Strathgordon.

Nicky wasn't in his bed.

She saw that first, and turned on the light, which told her only that the bed was, yes, completely empty. The curtains were closed. She walked to the window and uncovered it, half expecting to find it broken, and Nicky gone again, but the window was intact.

A chair stood nearby, and she put her hand on it, suspended. Was he in the bathroom? His door hadn't been barricaded.

Then she saw that the drape on one side bulged. She touched it, and saw one draw-cord stretched tight; she jerked the drape aside.

And screamed.

Nicky sat against the wall, legs folded under him, his head cocked sideways. The cord was around his neck.

Marti pounced, hoisted him up, and grabbed for the knot. He didn't move. She forced her fingers under the loop, and couldn't drop him down again to strangle, so she savagely tore the cord loose from its mechanism and ran with the limp child down the hall.

He wasn't in rigor mortis. He was warm.

They were gone, driven away, and she ran with him out of the house, leaving the door ajar. She put him in the front seat–no time to call an ambulance–leaped into the Mazda, slid under the wheel, his head on her lap. She whipped the little car around and down the drive. Thank God she knew the way to the nearest hospital.

Thank God the loop was loose around his neck every time she touched it. Thank God he'd fallen down to the floor, had not been dangling.

Thank God he coughed, and tried to turn over where he lay. Only then she started weeping. Thank you, Nicky, thank you, God. Oh, God, thank you!

Joel

He'd never been so furious. Joel Dalton shook so hard that it was a good thing he had the quarter-mile jog to his car, parked out of sight of the house. When he got in, he still retained the sensation of Nicky's four limbs, hanging on with amazing strength, but getting no help from him. Or protection. His pompous, heartless, self-righteous father!

"Like my father," Joel told himself. "Like my own father's life!"

He started the engine and leaned back, arms braced on the wheel, elbows locked. He blew out air hissing through his teeth. His father had suffered like that until a luckier child took him in hand, took his hands in hers; almost literally unbound him. Nicky had actually been tied up. Did those things still happen? Not in years had he heard of such unimaginable atrocities. And he went hunting for them, nose to the ground. Atrocity-hunter. This case came to him, fell into his lap, the girl in the cafe so concerned, afraid to confide in him.

He couldn't drive if he kept on thinking like this. Auschwitz-thoughts. He drove and drove, and found himself near the Inn.

The restaurant was already hot and dark, closed since eight. He knew he couldn't sleep, not after that blow-up and his continuing red rage, so he slung on an apron and went into the kitchen, flicking on the lights as he went, scuffing angrily past freezers and racks of dishes Ginny had done for tomorrow. Hot as Hades now, and he'd have to up the temperature, baking for tomorrow. He opened all the windows. No cool dawn to bake in, before the breakfast crowd, but he knew that tonight he'd never sleep. Bake now and sleep later. Until he had to open the place at six-thirty. Don't think about Nicky. "Nicky," not "Nickie." He'd been corrected; what a game little kid! True grit. Forget him for awhile.

The Wander Inn was sure some fancy name for a five-booth, eight-stool cafe, but the food was good, thanks to him and to Mom's recipes. He'd laid a nice imitation oak floor of congoleum and paneled the place. No artificial flowers, no plastic or chrome. College people don't go for that. Live plants, lots of wood–okay, so all of it wasn't real wood, but the door- and window-frames were, and the counter-edges.

He hadn't told Marti that two other guys put up the capital, and he furnished the muscle to earn his third of the profits. They were lawyers he'd gone through U. Tenn. with, and didn't know how to bake pies and bread. Like this.

Cooking was becoming a pain in the neck. He finally had decided to go back to school, but not necessarily in Special Ed. He had a right to choose his career. He was sick of hearing people say he must use his "inbred talent," and not waste it, "disgracefully."

"A Native Signer? Working as a cafe cook? Terrible!"

Native Signers were at a premium, nowadays. Not book-trained, second-language signers. English was his second language. His own peculiar way of gesturing as he talked, he supposed, was his "accent."

"I'll be what I want to be," he grumped to himself.

Good old cops, to clue him in about Nicky, look in their books for the Strathgordon name and address. He was always the one dragged to police stations and hospitals to interpret, and probably he would've been called in on Nicky's case, too, if Marti hadn't beaten him to it. A week ago. Exactly a week ago he'd run. It should've been this restaurant Nicky ran to, except they weren't open all night, like the other place.

He went out to the phone before he got all floured up, and called Marti's number. No one answered. Then he dialed the Strathgordon number and found no one there, either. Odd.

Joel slapped oil, milk, and flour into an enormous bowl, kneading it with hands scrubbed absolutely clean. Like white flesh, with a sweet, fleshy smell to it, but one heck of an unhealthy color. She was brown as he was, almost, and she ran. Nice. He'd been a lot more interested in Nicky than in Marti, but he hadn't missed everything.

Peaches into one pie-shell, blueberries into another, and apples sliced into numbers three and four.

"I do want to go back to school," he told himself (not adding the other things he wanted, at twenty-nine). "School for me, not for them. Not that I could ever hope to out-do Superbrother."

He washed his hands at ten o'clock and phoned her house again. Still not home. Was she spending the night with some guy? And where was Nicholas Strathgordon? What did they do to him after he left? And to her? She'd been holding both hands over her mouth when he last saw her, when he left–like in an old movie: struck dumb.

"Get out of my house!" was plenty theatrical, too.

So was Nicky. Poor little Nicky.

At ten-thirty, he decided to pack it in. He'd maybe drive past her house, her cousin's house, where she wouldn't be for much longer. If a light was on, he'd go in. Try to get in. Ask what happened out there after he left.

He was at his car before he remembered to go back in and fetch the eclairs he'd baked yesterday, for Marti to give to Nicky.

Marti

Nicky hadn't roused much. His energy seemed to be concentrated in a few little fingers that clung to her knee.

A child-suicide. What can you say? Think? Nicky ran away—voted with his feet—and when they nailed shut his escape-hatch, they were nailing shut his coffin.

Almost.

Hildegaard crawled from the back seat over Nicky, and sat on the floor beside Nicky, sniffing him with interest. Her bulk kept him from sliding off the seat. Joel. Tell Joel? But his coming caused this. Nicky might have stuck it out for ten more days til Mama came back and snatched him home to Pittsburgh. But he'd seen his father throw Joel out, and where did that leave Nicky? Did Nicky know it would last only ten more days? How could he know? No one told him anything, even in written notes. That was "illegal."

She said a very bad word.

"How do you feel?" she asked the silent child lying along the front seat. "We're going straight to the doctor."

What happens if you jump from a chair with a cord noosed around your throat? Had the heavy drapes been closed when they put him to bed? No. No, she remembered muttering to Annalee about those nails visible in the windowframe, while the woman undressed Nicky. His leap had jerked the drapes closed, so he hadn't snapped his neck. In this fading light, she couldn't judge the severity of the rope-burn around his neck. She'd sure preserve the looped cord for proof. Of what Joel called "child-abuse."

Find an emergency room. She pictured horrified nurses, popping flashbulbs, police and reporters. That would likely mean more harm to Nicky than to the parents who deserved public humiliation. Nicky didn't. He needed peace and quiet. And someone to talk to.

He was staring up at her, head in her lap, eyes focused, hands lying limp on his stomach. Waiting for her to do him some good, if she was so smart.

What had Joel taught her? Strike your forehead and point to yourself. Circle your fist on your chest.

"Stupid, me," she signed one-handed, as she drove.

"Me sorry."

Then, "I-love-you."

He stared.

Oh, God. Was he over the edge? Brain-damaged? Gone quietly mad? Who could blame him? But not now. "Not yet, Nicky! We've got a life for you to live, Nicky. Seventy more years or so."

"Look," she mouthed to him, "I'm TALKING ON MY HANDS!"

At a stop-light, she ran through her three lines again, and then wracked her memory for some of the signs from that TV sermon. "Jesus" she remembered, and "Bible," but how about "Help"? "Help you"? "Me help you"?

His lashes flickered.

"Hildegaard," she said, "DO something besides sit there."

Hildegaard obeyed. While Marti drove, she leaned across Nicky's legs and began industriously licking his hands. Candy-hands, probably sticky from Annalee's sweet glop. Hildie put a paw on the edge of the seat, reached further, and licked his chin til he grimaced and pushed her down. He tried to sit up.

Marti pulled over, opened the glove compartment and got out a hunting-knife in a sheath. She worked fast, behind the boy's head, so he wouldn't see, and managed to saw through the cord. At last. Then she quickly flung the severed loop and trailing six-foot cord into the back seat of the Mazda, out of sight.

To the hospital.

He sat up, signing to her, frowning; not attempting, for once, to talk, and she dug in the glove compartment again for a stub of pencil and a road map. She gave them to him.

"Run," was all he could scribble.

He didn't want to see a doctor.

Then she remembered something else. The hospital meant other things besides scandal for the Strathgordons and vindication for Joel. It meant Nicky would surely go back to live with Daddy.

Call his family in Pittsburgh! That's what she'd do. Nicky was not in any condition to be questioned, so she found a phone booth, called long-distance information in Pittsburgh, and went limp with relief to learn that "Strathgordon" was listed. Only one of them. Good.

She'd have to call collect and argue someone into accepting her call—but when she dialed, the telephone rang a dozen times. No one home. She could telephone the grandparents who'd been keeping Nicky—somewhere in Kentucky?—but she could remember neither the city or their name. Nicky's mother's folks, those were, not Strathgordons.

She got back into the car, totally at a loss. Where to turn?

Saturday night, and her marathon was next Saturday. She was due to stay here, house-sitting, til Wednesday, but cats can feed themselves from an open bin. Leave them water. Leave a note for Susan, leave this car. Take Nicky somewhere? Tuck him into her bed over the cab and head for Pittsburgh, right now? Vanish? Leave the Strathgordon's door standing open into the night, the cord missing from the drape, Nicky missing, let them call the police– Oh, heavens! The police!

Her heart was racing as if she were sprinting. Don't get carried away by the excitement of it. Slow down. Think. Thank your lucky stars you wore jeans tonight with your wallet in your pocket. No purse left behind in that house. No loose ends. She hadn't wanted the port wine and sponge cake left there on the table.

Then she remembered Joel, again. She must phone him, and let him know what she was doing. He'd approve. He'd keep her out of prison; he knew policemen, his dear friends.

First, she had to make Nicky happy.

She wrote on the margin of the road-map, "We are going home to Pittsburgh. NOW."

He turned a beaming face up to her.

No, he was not brain-damaged. Just winded and desperate and frightened half to death. She put her fingers on his neck and manipulated it, rocking his head carefully forward, to each side, and back. He didn't wince or complain. Nothing broken. "You feel OK?" she wrote, and he nodded yes. He had a teenage brother and two sisters in Pittsburgh. Until Mama came home, she could surely entrust him to them. If only they'd been home. But what a shock for kids to be told, "Your baby brother just hanged himself."

They might not even trust a strange woman; they might call Lanier and report her. Nicky couldn't vouch for her, over a telephone.

Joel. No, call Joel.

Nicky raised his brows and said "Ol?" He must have seen her lips. His hand rose thoughtfully to the side of his neck, and he fingered the skin, brow creased as if he didn't remember what had scored the soft flesh. She smoothed the hair down over premature worry-lines in his brow, saying, "There, darling. I love you."

Thank heavens that one hand-shape was so easy.

"I love you. I love you, Nicky."

He stretched his arms up around her neck, and she hugged him.

Hildegaard took that opportunity to ooze surreptiously up onto the passenger seat.

"Hey! That's Nicky's seat. We have to go now, Nicky."

He leaned against Hildegaard as if she were a warm, panting pillow.

Marti drove more carefully and slowly now through the dark, ferrying her precious cargo to the next gas station she could find.

She left Hildie as babysitter and in the phone booth looked up "Dalton, Joel." She dialed his number, but he wasn't home.

Darn him! Sitting in some bar, somewhere, she bet, brooding, when Nicky needed him. The Wander Inn closed at eight, he said. If it reopened at seven tomorrow morning, she might reach him there, or must she phone his home number every hour, from further and further east of Knoxville?

She next checked the map. To reach Pittsburgh would take her twelve hours.

The only sure thing was that Nicky must not fall into his father's hands. Next time he'd stab himself to death, do a thorough job of it. Or stick a knife in someone else.

In vain, she tried Joel's number again, and the Pittsburgh Strathgordons; groaning, Marti checked Nicky, sleeping in the Mazda. Go to Joel's residence? Look on the wall-map in the station to find Laurel Avenue?

She did, and she drove to the right street, but Joel's small house was dark. She even knocked, and no one answered.

No more delay. She had to hurry home and switch vehicles, pack in a rush, stick her suitcases and race-supplies into the camper and clear out. Lucky her, mobile; her whole house on wheels behind and above her.

Don't let the Strathgordons find them. Or the police. Better to go in Susan's car? No, Lanier could trace that from Susan's address, and drag her cousin into this. Stick with the camper.

Nicky was cramped, so she put him in the back seat with a raincoat rolled up as a pillow. She no longer handled him gingerly, for fear he'd break, or as if a little boy had bristles or thorns. He felt as familiar to her hands, now, as Hildegaard.

Nicky didn't fall straight to sleep again. He seized Marti's hand, forcing her fingers open, and propped it on her cheek by her thumb.

"Mama" he said.

"Marti," she said, afraid she'd start sniveling. "My name is Marti. Joel told you." Pointing to herself. She took his sneakers off.

He raised his hand and fluttered fingers at her, then pointed at her, his finger poking her chest. "You." "You . . . flutter-flutter."

She'd have to work on this in daylight.

She had so much to learn.

Joel

Where the heck WAS she? Was everyone?

Past eleven, and she wasn't home yet to answer her phone. Maybe she'd looked him up in the phone book and was sitting parked outside his house? She hadn't called or shown up at the cafe. He drove home, but found no Mazda. Or camper. No answer at the Strathgordon place, either.

It made him angry. He wanted to talk to her, teach her some sense. She had access to Nicky, and he never would. Not after blasting Strathgordon. His lies, he hoped, at least had saved her from blame.

She had to leave Knoxville soon. He kept forgetting her marathon over in Pine Mountain, North Caroline, that once upon a time he'd considered entering. It was next Saturday, and she'd leave here Wednesday, she said. Leave Nicky to people who crucified him. He knew what she'd say, "Why are you so incensed about it?"

He'd tell her to picture the son of an Auschwitz-victim meeting a neo-Nazi. Of course he blew his cool, yelled, wanted to kill. He'd all his life collected horror-stories, and lived through others. His father's parents had never said a thing understandable to their deaf son. They'd just pushed him and hit him to communicate. And then they dared, years later, to come bearing gifts to visit the grandson who could hear.

At six years old he was glad he'd had the guts to say, "Daddy doesn't even know you, so I don't need you, either."

Nicky, thank God, had a signing mother. He signed almost as fluently as the child of a deaf mother, but English kept creeping in. He'd gotten that from her, those English constructions and syntax.

Joel shook his head, eyes closed, sitting in his Chevy in front of the Wander Inn, without a place to go. Nicky. Strathgordon was going to keep torturing him. He'd have to call the rest of the family in Pittsburgh, that Nicky told him about. He'd never seen a kid talk so much, so fast. As for his voice–listen hard to Nicky for a week and you'd catch a lot. His voice was far above average.

If he knew which were Nicky's windows, he'd go out there and creep up the grassy hill on foot, break in, and kidnap the kid. No, Nicky said his window was nailed shut. Damn! And you can't go around a house tapping on windowpanes to wake a deaf kid, even if you can get the window open to pull him out.

Where was Marti? He circled the block, drove home, and phoned her again. No luck. Back out to the freeway and down to Magnolia. She didn't have anyone in town to bunk with, she said.

He could suggest somebody.

No lights were on in her house. Were the police wrong about her address, that they'd given him along with Nicky's? What could he do for Nicky, anyway? Was he running after Nicky for Nicky's sake, or for his own? Or to get to Marti?

Driving back toward the main drag, again, Joel put on the brakes.

A small camper sat over there at the curb, like Nicky described. Hers? She'd had a Mazda tonight at Strathgordon's house. Indiana plates. So that wasn't the house? This one was?

He started to go up to the door before something told him not to. It isn't legal any longer to fire through your front door before opening it, but it pays to be careful.

Peering into the camper, he stood on the small step to the back door. The truck, top-heavy with camper, rocked a bit.

At the door, a small face appeared, illuminated by a flashlight.

"Nicky?" Nicky!

He rattled the door, hissing, "Hey, let me IN! How'd you get Nicky?"

She unlocked the door, practically pulling him inside, hushing him. "Come, look what they did to Nicky!"

He joined them on the wide bed over the cab, falling across the big dog to get there, and clutched onto Nicky. Nicky clutched him in return. She didn't flash the light around. They communicated by speech and feel. Sit here. Her voice was soft and furious, but not at him. Taking Nicky's hand, he spelled into the palm a few reassurances while he listened to Marti.

Then he stopped spelling and sat there dumbfounded.

"Holy God in heaven! It couldn't— He didn't— What are you trying to say? That he tried to- He attempted suicide? Nicky did?"

That's what she was trying to say, talking fast, Yankee-fashion, and he broke in.

"We'll take him away. Far away, and never tell them!" "Can you?" "Yes, but—" "We must; you must; the police must—" "Oh, God, Joel, we have to get him out of town, back to Mama—" "I will." "You will?" "Trust me, I will," he said.

They must head for Pittsburgh that minute. Split. With a dog along, and a kid that wasn't theirs. Joel put his arm around Marti and found out how hard she was shaking.

"It's really hitting me, now," she whispered.

He wondered it didn't hit her before. Tough cookie. She'd had to pack and leave a bunch of cats comfortable. She'd been calling him, but not at the Inn. Her phone had rung and rung, but for fear it was Strathgordon, she couldn't answer it. The Mazda was stashed in Sue's garage, and she'd parked out of sight of the house, to foil searchers. She'd almost foiled him. Another three minutes, and she would have been gone.

"Does he need a doctor, Joel?"

He didn't think so. No time. He said, "Let's clear out. Get out of their reach. "Police, though?" "We can telephone Strathgordon and threaten exposure, if he calls them."

She nodded, still seized by startling spells of trembling. Not that he wasn't a bit shaky himself, and sick to his stomach.

"Let's go," he said, but when he tried to make his way out of the camper, he stepped on the immense dog, which yelped.

"I need her, traveling alone at night," Marti explained.

After he grabbed the eclairs and the change of clothing—always kept in his car for after running, he locked up the Chevy and walked around the corner to check the house. Past midnight, and he had a feeling Strathgordon wouldn't just sit back and let Nicky disappear.

Marti was behind the wheel, now, and Nicky in the bed above her head.

That's when he heard a motor. Thinking she was driving around the corner to fetch him, he stood in full view on the moonlit sidewalk. Then he realized the sound came from the direction of Magnolia.

He dodged toward the corner, looked back, and then sprinted for the camper.

Strathgordon's blue Cordova was easing along the curb in front of Marti's cousin's house.

He fled down the block and leaped into the truck beside Marti, forcing her away from the wheel.

"Let's go! You've got company up ahead. I wanna drive."

"Oh, no! Not him!"

"It was his Cordova. We gotta move it fast."

He backed the truck, made a U-turn in the middle of the street, and headed east. Would Strathgordon follow the engine he must hear and the headlights he'd see, if he came around the corner?

"We can fix things by phone, once we've lost him," Joel said. "Got the kid out of his reach."

"But what about you?" she asked him, when he'd driven a few miles. "Your car? Can you dash off like this? I took time to bring everything I have, plus food from the refrigerator."

"Don't worry about me. I'm pretty much at liberty; they'll get a sub for me at the cafe. Strathgordon probably didn't even catch my name, and he won't know my car. He'll blame you for taking Nicky. We've got to fix that, fast. Call the cops ourselves, before they put out an APB."

"A what?"

"All-Points Bulletin. Pull you over before we hit North Carolina."

"But we're going to Pennsylvania."

"That's what we'll say. But Nicky's Mom isn't home, yet, you said. If Strathgordon rushes right up here—well, he can lay claim to the kid by default. Let's keep Nicky out of his hands, if you want Nicky to stay alive."

"Of course I do!"

"Then trust me. Marti, I've been mixed up in things worse than this, gettin' caught between deaf people and cops, deaf people and lawyers, creditors, doctors, the whole crazy mixup. It's perpetual. I've had guys take a swing at me, I've been sued—you name it. But get a damned good police chief and a sheriff on your side, like I've got in Knoxville, and there's leeway."

"I . . . see."

They were pushing sixty on the Asheville Highway. He found a little hamlet where he knew there was a phone booth, and left the road so abruptly Marti came slewing over against him; a pleasant feeling.

He used his telephone credit-card to call the police department, and talked to a pair of cops he knew. He explained what Strathgordon might say and do. No, the father didn't have legal custody. You might say that he—Joel—was a representative of the absent mother, who did have custody.

(That would hold them.) He 'd go to the mother's place. He'd call and keep them posted, so just cool off the father and discourage any police action, okay? His responsibility. As for the baby-sitter, Marti Hanson, she wasn't involved. At all. No, the kid wasn't beaten or abused; he tried to off himself. Kill himself. No injuries resulted. The next time, he said, who knows? He's a deaf child.

He hoped that would hold them, the mystery of what to do with a deaf child. He didn't have many of them signing, yet, in the department.

Now to make sure Strathgordon didn't try to force the cops' hand.

He called Nicky's father, but got only the wife, the featherheaded Kewpie-doll, and told her Nicky attempted suicide but now was safe with him. Marti? Not involved. Sit tight. When Nicky's mother came back to Pittsburgh, she'd have Nicky, safe and sound. Right now, Nicky needed him, Joel Dalton. (Remember me?) Any complaints from Nicky's dad, and Nicky might not reappear for quite some time. Dad might even land in jail for child-abuse.

No, it was not a kidnapping.

He knew he sounded like a tough TV detective, but it worked. She started blubbering, and then begging, and promised to keep Strathgordon quiet. He was out searching for Marti and Nicky; he'd call her again any minute.

"I've already called the cops," Joel said in conclusion. "You can think of me sorta like a cop, too. Child-Protective variety."

When he hung up, he was surprised how weak his legs were. He actually limped back to the truck, but he persuaded Marti to let him drive again.

Next stop, he'd call Bill Crane and tell him to get a substitute cook. For a week. Till further notice.

Pine Mountain was near Skyline Drive and the Virginia line, up high. Beautiful country. Had she told Nicky's folks where she was holding her marathon? Be nice to know that.

Marti said they'd never asked.

"Leave everything to me," he soothed her. "We've got the cops on our side, Strathgordon hadn't even reported you two missing, yet, and finding no Mazda must have put him off our scent. Nobody's followed us. A Cordova could have overtaken this rig in no time."

"I don't like to play cops and robbers," she said in a very small voice.

"I hate to admit it, but I do," he said cheerfully. "Strathgordon's wife was a push-over. She's probably delighted to get rid of Nicky, and once he thinks about the alternatives I offered: scandal or jail, he will be, too."

"So we give Nicky back to his mother? When she gets home?"

"Right. That's not my idea, it's yours, remember? You've just got yourself a chauffeur you didn't plan on, and defense against any legal problems."

"I'm glad." she said, and looked at him for a long time, so he could feel her eyes examining his profile.

He left the highway over the state line in North Carolina's Pisgah Forest and pulled into the deserted end of a campground. Locking up the cab, supporting Marti with one crooked arm, he went around the camper and boosted her in through the back door. Bedtime. All the conveniences of a house, here. Without a word—did she think their sleeping Nicky could hear?—she reached into a styrofoam cooler and handed him a beer.

There was even a midget latrine on board, and, right outside, a comfort station.

They sat facing each other in the dark across a table, the way they had the first time they met. He drank the beer, she drank a Dr. Pepper. Nicky, up in the bed, snored. The dog at his feet sniffed him endlessly, smelling food. They didn't talk.

Running shoes shed, they climbed up to join Nicky, one on each side. What was it in the old King Arthur stories, about chaste lovers sleeping with a naked sword between them? Nicky served the same purpose, except a sword doesn't snore. You sure couldn't tell that this sleeping Nicky was deaf. As some would say, a "deaf-mute."

It was a queen-size bed. Nicky roused and required soothing in the dark, holding Joel's wrists as he signed where they were and how wonderful everything was; no, Daddy would never catch him. Pittsburgh was their destination.

Eventually.

Marti went right off to sleep, or she pretended to, as he settled down on his third of the mattress, for comfort taking off only his belt, after emptying his pockets.

A nice bed, but he couldn't sleep much. The dog down on the floor scratched fleas and shook the camper. He kept thinking about Marti Hanson, and the guts she had. And about the pleasure of his revenge. As for Nicky, Nicky didn't snore any more, but Nicky's twitchy little legs kept running, running, and running.

All night long.

Marti

Marti would turn her camper over to Joel at Pine Mountain.

That's what they finally decided, waking up in the forest, staring at each other across the sleeping child.

"I won't have you involved in this," he said. "I told the cops you were not with me, so if they check, and I'm a liar, there goes my credibility."

"You'll go right straight on to Pittsburgh?" she asked him. "As for me, yeah, without wheels I can survive in a very small town."

"And you're a runner."

He lay on his side, propping his head on his hand. Her response, she noticed, seemed to please him greatly.

"Pittsburgh's still a long way north of Pine Mountain," Marti said. "Go fast as you can, or you'll have to call again to reassure Nicky's father and the police and everyone."

"I'm not talking to his father. Let him stew."

"Better let Nicky's brother and sisters know he's coming, though. Maybe they can get word to his mother where he is. Her name's Jane. Janie."

"Remember, she went off and deserted Nicky," Joel retorted. "And the grandparents—they gave him up to that louse of a father. I wouldn't worry about THEM, either."

Marti sighed, staring at his fiercely earnest face. So angry! She'd never tire of watching its changing expressions; she believed Joel mainly because of his face. A perfect face was pretty, but boring. A mask.

Nicky kept his own face smothered against her, and she left her hand on his side to make sure he still was breathing. Joel went down into the truck and drove.

They reached Pine Mountain before noon, and she directed him to her race-assistants' house.

"This'll be the last I'll ever see of Nicky," she mused, moist around the eyes.

"You don't want a deaf kid, do you?"

His tone of voice surprised her. Sarcasm, challenge, appeal—

"Not just any deaf kid, no. Not just any kid, for that matter. But Nicky—he grows on you. And when he can understand me, and I can understand him—"

She woke up suddenly to a wider perspective on their situation.

"We really are kidnappers, you know that?"

"Sure," he cracked. "I'd like to see every deaf kid born to hearies be given to deaf couples to raise."

"We are not a deaf couple," she said. "And that's a sick idea. After all!"

"You saw what happened to Nicky. Suppose Daddy got custody of him?"

She didn't tell him that Daddy planned to fight for custody of Nicky. She remembered Alan.

"I've met a born-deaf man with good speech, a good job at TVA—"

"I've never met a guy like that, in Knoxville."

"Well, there's—"

"Let's split up," he said, interrupting her. "I see your friend out on her porch now, looking curious. Let's not give her anything to wonder about."

Marti slid out of the truck, and they went around to the camper.

"I've got lots of boxes to unload," she said. "And my suitcases. You can keep all the food. I can tie Hildie in their back yard, I suppose."

"Won't take long. Tell me where to put things."

She checked with Mrs. McCoy, who motioned toward their garage, standing open, already stocked with bushel baskets of multicolored banners, drink-containers, and boxes of ERG.

The McCoys had insisted Marti use their guest room, so the absence of her camper would make no difference; Joel would soon be back. Give him a day to Pittsburgh, a day there, and a day to return, and he'd hit Pine Mountain again about Thursday, the day after she'd expected to arrive. Her hostess took their early arrival in stride.

When Marti had nothing of hers left on board, she went into the camper to say goodbye to Nicky.

"You like sad partings?" Joel asked.

"No. I almost wish we wouldn't wake him up."

"He'd never have slept through so much rocking and bumping if he weren't pretty wrecked, emotionally," Joel observed. He'll need lots of rest and quiet, to recover. He may not even remember the suicide-attempt."

"Don't tell him, then."

"I won't. That's a job for a psychiatrist, if there was such a thing."

"What do you mean?"

"Find me one signing psychiatrist."

"Oh."

They climbed up to the bed again, Joel with a paper bag in his hand. He woke Nicky by passing a chocolate-frosted, cream-filled eclair back and forth under the boy's nose. Nicky rose up onto his elbows and grabbed at it.

"See? Hits the spot," Joel said. "And one for you, and one for me. Lunch."

"Did you make these?"

"Sure."

"They're delicious."

Nicky was watching them over his eclair, chocolate-faced, big-eyed and busy chewing. Joel tousled his hair. They had hair the same color of brown, Joel's wavier than Nicky's and not feather-cut like the boy's. Both sat on the mattress cross-legged. Marti never mentioned the bright pink line encircling Nicky's throat.

"Don't look so sad. It's not the end of the world," Joel said. Have a nice marathon."

"You'll be back here long before then! That's not til Saturday! Hey, I want my camper back Thursday, at least. Don't make the round-trip without sleeping in between, of course, but . . . Joel, can I trust you? I really don't know a thing about you."

"If the cops trust me, you don't?"

"Well . . . you get so vindictive."

"I know. Toward those who deserve it. Trust me," he said in his slow drawling baritone, "to do what's best for Nicky. To hell with the rest of them."

He took her hand and squeezed it, as if in happier circumstances he'd kiss it—or her—goodbye. She pulled Nicky over and hugged him.

"Tell him I love him."

"You can sign that, yourself."

So she did.

"Tell him he's wonderful, and he'll be all right, and I'm sorry we let it go on as long as it did. Daddy won't get him, again."

"You tell him that. Just do what I do." Joel said.

He positioned Nicky so the boy faced Marti, and when Joel signed, Marti fumblingly followed his signs, one by one. She knew "sorry" when it came. Nicky nodded and nodded, not smiling, taking it all in.

What more to say? "Thanks," she told Joel, thinking how much more inconvenienced he was by all this than she. "Please, you're both valuable. Drive carefully. It drinks unleaded gas."

"Happy race," he said, and off he went. They went.

She felt like dropping down on the green lawn and crying, but she couldn't.

"Marti? Have you eaten any lunch, yet, Marti?"

Hildie was yanking on her leash, and little Mrs. McCoy was upon her.

She knew the best antidote for grief, and today she had it. Running. And tomorrow and tomorrow and tomorrow. Directing a race.

Tom McCoy had run the 1927 Boston Marathon, back when hundreds, not tens of thousands of Americans raced twenty-six miles. He and his wife were her chief assistants and her favorite Pine Mountaineers. He lined up in a shining brigade on the diningroom table the gold and silver trophies she'd brought. They showed her stacks of hand-lettered numbers for runners' chests. On their wall hung a map, in water-colors, of her loop course along the ridge of Pine Mountain. No Heartbreak Hills at her marathons. The deadly last six miles were, if possible, flat or a net downhill.

The chemical toilets had not yet been heard from.

"Maybe we can truck in some little privies, down from the hills," she said, her urban Yankee humor not much appreciated.

When should cameras and the press be told to arrive? The mile-record was what? A little under four minutes. Men now ran twenty-six miles at about 5:00 each. No, less, she said. Jock Stead, premier hill-runner from California, was happening by, so call it a 2:20 marathon, and 2:50 for the first woman. Two hours and fifty minutes.

She wished Joel could run, but he claimed to be out of shape, as well as otherwise employed. He had that vital little errand, that package for Pittsburgh. (Fast, fast, fast, before some parent suffered apoplexy.)

She unpacked her brand new bullhorn from its UPS box, and then sat down to letter "RACE OFFICIAL" through a stencil on a dozen brilliant yellow vests. Traffic controllers. A first race was home-made, hand-made, but that meant everyone was innocent, teachable, and afterwards delighted with her beautiful racers. Don't think about Nicky. Don't think about deafness. Or Joel. Or, for that matter, Lanier Strathgordon or Alan Teague, gnashing teeth back in Knoxville.

That night, Marti put herself to bed at eight and slept til noon. During the next three days she was taken on scenic mountain drives, stuffed with delicious food in four different homes, and made much of. She ran, daily, with Hildie by her side. She telephoned cousin Susan to give her a well-laundered version of the Nicky story, explaining why she wasn't there to greet them on their return from New York.

The toilets arrived. Everything arrived but Joel, in her camper. No call from him, either, but she'd neglected to give him the number, and there were five McCoys in the tiny local phone book.

Friday, half her runners came to town to pick up their packets, and Saturday morning she was up at five, fretting about Joel's absence. Well, it might even be a good sign. Maybe the Pittsburgh Strathgordons had taken him to their bosom for returning their kid and their brother.

Maybe he'd stolen her truck?

In the cool of morning, she ran back and forth among registrants lined up at tables by age and sex, making change, distributing pencils, and greeting friends met at past races. One was big Mike Curran, who gave her a wink, a pat on the rear, and a thumbs-up sign. "See you after the race, Doll." Just like always.

Probably those darned Porters would show up at the last minute, too late for her to try and persuade the mother not to enter a child in the race, the infant wonder, aged four.

She got her next surprise of the morning, a happy shock, when a school band, startling in gold and magenta uniforms, materialized around a bend in the road. Lining up near the starting line, they blasted into "The Camptown Races." This seldom happened, a race begun to music, and Marti's adrenaline surged. With that sort of send-off, SHE might be able to complete a marathon. In about ten hours, anyway.

The roadway was filling up with bright running shoes—foot-shaped Easter eggs with chartreuse, gold, fuschia, yellow, red, and orange stripes. Marti couldn't stop grinning in satisfaction. Her own green and purple shoes beat time with the drums, and she had to look twice at the attractive young blonde carrying her packet in her teeth, stooping to pin a number on a tiny . . . platinum-haired . . . yes, girl-child, in red singlet and shorts identical to her mother's.

Boy, she didn't want them to race unnoticed, did she?

"Mrs. Porter?" Marti inquired, wishing she looked like that. The child must be closer to three than to four. "Cute costumes," she began, "but Kim's so tiny. She must be allowed to drop out, if she tires."

The woman glowered.

"You see we're legally registered and running. You can't prevent it."

"What's Kim's projected time?" Marti cracked, only joking.

"A five-thirty," she replied.

(Only a toddler's world-record?)

The child was a doll. A wind-up doll, that is. Mother and daughter running Barbie dolls. Mother's ego was this dependent upon a child's performance?

That's when she spotted another kid, and he looked just like Nicky.

It was Nicky.

When he saw her across the beflagged course, he flashed her a weak grin—before a pack of runners jogged between them.

"Nickee!" she shrilled, shouldering her way through rainbows of T-shirts. "Why aren't you in Pittsburgh? How can you be here? Where's Joel?" (God, Oh, God, what's going on, here?)

He got the last word: "Ol." Eyes brightening, he pointed.

Blast Joel! There he stood, in sagging jeans and a blue T-shirt, looking Mrs. Porter up and down.

"Joel? You're back?" Only that, when she could have hit him. "Why isn't Nicky in Pittsburgh?"

He didn't answer immediately. She could have shaken him, but people kept jarring them apart in the crush of three hundred entrants.

"Mama's not home yet. Nicky didn't want to go home. We decided to come see your race."

"So what, if she's not home! Where on earth have you been since last Sunday?"

"Sightseeing in the mountains. Therapy for Nicky." He didn't sign.

"Did you keep his father informed?" she demanded, fending off questioners who'd spotted her as the head honcho, fending off their "have we time to hit the john?" "Are splits given at the ten and twenty?" "How about some Cokes at the aid-stations?"

"He doesn't deserve to be kept informed," said Joel. "He nearly killed Nicky."

"It's been SIX days, though. Joel, you are a KIDNAPPER!"

Her last word was drowned out by "The Stars and Stripes Forever."

The next thing she heard from Joel was, "I'm gonna jog your race. Unofficially."

"Who'll look after Nicky? I'll be terribly busy."

"He's nine. He can look after himself."

"But he's DEAF!"

Joel glared at her in disgust. "Oh, come off it!"

He was slipping out of his jeans, revealing his running shorts underneath. He handed the jeans to Nicky, who sent Marti a proud, possessive look.

"There's a four-year-old girl running," Marti gasped, after they heard the starter's pistol. The pack of runners began bouncing up and down, as speedsters in front sprinted away, leaving space for the mob to follow.

"FOUR?" Joel's furiously indignant face turned toward her, just as she expected.

"Over there, with Mama, in red. Keep an eye on her, will you?"

"It's a crime to let her run!"

Marti trotted alongside Joel, at the rear of the pack. "I couldn't prevent it."

He called Kim Porter's mother a very rude name, and then he was gone, running. Nicky stood with Joel's jeans hung over his shoulder, applauding. He looked as if he were cheering for his very own father.

Nicky

He was to help Marti. Joel told him to. Said he MUST. "Stay good," he signed, in American Sign Language, spelled "A-S-L." Nicky smiled at that. ASL was fast and beautiful and exciting, and English signs more like reading. Joel kept asking, "How you learn signs?" and he also asked, "Who deaf, your family?" "Who told you?" "How you know?" It was funny to see Joel shake his head because Nicky knew so much. Why not? Hearies do.

Sure, he'd stay good. First he walked around the cardtable with all the trophies on it. Joel had explained them. The fastest people get them, old people and young people each their own statue. Everyone got T-shirts that said "Pine Mountain," but only fastests got statues. Flags were blowing in the air, red, green, yellow, and blue, rows and rows of them, which was pretty. Like little clothes on a clothesline. He bet they rang like bells.

He jumped when he felt the push on his face and neck. The big drum was beating. Almost tall as he was, and it said "Pine Mountain High School." The trumpets were gold in the sun, and he pretended they said "toot-toot" loud enough to hear. He took out the notebook Joel bought him with spirals where Joel tied the string. (Joel used teeth to dent the pencil all around to hold on the loop of the string.)

Nicky wanted to live with Joel forever.

They'd walked through runners bending over and putting goo on toes and legs and tying bands around their heads, to get to the band. The man with the long, black horn had frowned and jerked back when Nicky stuck out his hand to touch music. So he went to the girl with shiny silver squares hanging, like a xylophone standing on its head.

"May I touch it?" he said, very clear, when she stopped hammering, and she opened mouth "O" and looked around, and the others looked at him and smiled and made flutter-mouths.

She put his hand on the silver music-machine, and when she hammered the next time, it felt so funny he laughed. The big drum hit his face nice, boom, boom, and he tapped his foot like everyone else.

Joel said the race was long, long, long, and took a long, long time. They had to line up, to start. Only it wasn't a line. It was a big bunch, all tight.

Marti carried a board on her arm. She was mad at Joel, and they talked fast.

Joel took off his pants, and Nicky got them.

A man up on a chair had a gun, but not a cop's gun. Nicky tried to listen hard; half sorry Joel let him take his hearing-aids off. He watched the gun-man's face, up above all the skinny, wiggly people with colored shoes and shirts. They wiggled their knees like they wanted bathroom, but the front ones leaned over with hands on knees and glared straight down the road.

The man raised the gun, straight up, ready to shoot at the moon.

Nicky looked at a little girl in red clothes with mother. Joel frowned at her mother.

Suddenly, people started running, mostly people in front, and in back they hopped up and down and made laugh-faces, til they could run, too.

At the end of all the people, he saw the little girl, again. She was holding her mother's hand, and they didn't run fast.

Joel didn't wave til he was almost out of sight. Then he looked back and signed, "No run away!"

When the runners all left, he saw Marti talking, talking, and old people piling up papers and pencils and jars of pins. It looked like carnival-time at school, afterwards. At clean-up. There were boxes and boxes and big green garbage cans, and lots of people talking, and none of these people had bare legs.

Marti looked so busy that he went over to her. He remembered she knew "help," so he did it and pointed to her. "Help you." She knelt down and hugged him, hard, and kissed him. Her face was pink-excited.

So he sat down to wait. Two hours, Joel said, but he didn't have a watch. He hoped Marti had a watch. A stopped-watch.

He could feel Marti watching him, but she didn't bother him. He lay back on the grass and looked at the trees near the sky. It wouldn't rain. It was bright sun, starting warm. At night in the camper Joel had a flashlight, so they could talk and talk til midnight and the battery died.

Then they went out and looked at the stars, and Nicky told Joel constellations. Miss Ferreir had given him a book of stars at school to learn. Joel said he knew a grown-up man who thought the stars were the sun shining through holes in a black curtain. The curtain came down at night. The man was deaf; Joel didn't say who he was. Joel said Nicky could teach them all about stars. Joel didn't know constellations like Pleiades, so Nicky named them.

He was sleepy all the next day.

They stopped by a stream, and Joel helped him build a dam to make a lake. TVA lake. Out of their milk cartons Joel cut pieces and made a waterwheel that turned. He did that, he said, when he was a little boy. He didn't have a little boy and he wanted one. His brother had a little boy. His brother was deaf like Joel's mama and daddy, and his brother's little boy was deaf, too. Nicky wanted to go see them, but they lived far away. His brother had a little girl, too. Joel's niece. She was a hearie. She was two, and the boy was six.

Nicky remembered asking, "When will you get a little boy?" and Joel said he didn't know. He needed to have a wife, first. Nicky said "Marti?" and Joel looked at him funny and hit him like play on the arm and didn't talk anymore, for awhile.

Joel asked was Nicky's mama's mama deaf, but Nicky said no. She was a hearie. Mama didn't want him anymore. He didn't want to think about her.

"Okay," Joel said, "Then we won't go to Pittsburgh."

They bought weiners and cheese and rolls and apples to make lunch, and Joel let him have a root beer. The next day they drove up high over clouds and stopped, and Joel put a bottle of orange juice and sandwiches in a bag, and they climbed up on Mt. LeConte. For hours and hours up to the top, more than a mile high, Joel said. Nicky didn't get tired, and Joel said that was like a marathon for him. It was like airplanes, looking down on the roads and cars and towns from the top, and going down was easy.

The next day they went to a town called Cherokee Indian, and Joel got Nicky moccasins and a hatchet, and let him talk to chiefs with black hair and eyes. They ate pizza there, and Nicky got six postcards and a Baby Ruth bar, and they talked and talked. About things.

At night mosquitos bit them, and Joel said they kept him awake, humming. Nicky was surprised. He knew bees buzz, but no one told him mosquitos have voices. "Flies, too." said Joel. "Imagine!" They stopped at a bakery and got more eclairs. Nicky liked them very much and had to wash face and hands in a stream afterwards in their campground with the bears. Big black bears.

Joel said his daddy and mama were getting a hearing-ear dog, to show when doorbell rang, and fire. That was better than flashings. Nicky wanted to meet that smart dog, and Joel said maybe someday.

When Nicky lifted his head, Marti was still running around talking into a cone and writing things and pointing. Where were the runners?

Kirby said runners hurt knees and catch bunions. Their shins have splints on them. He worried about Joel.

He went over and pointed to Marti's watch and then down the road and shaded his eyes, like hearies do, and said,"What time?" very clear. She wrote, "11:15 start watching for the winner." She showed it was eleven, so he said again, "Help you?"

She held him by the shoulder and led him to a long table with T-shirts in piles and old ladies sitting in chairs, and garbage cans and stacks of paper cups. They talked, Marti and them, and he wished she was smart enough to interpret.

Then she squatted down to his size and held up a cup and pointed to the ground and said, ". . . cup . . . pick up . . ."

He nodded. But he didn't see any cups on the ground.

Then she said something else and made drinking from cup, and threw it down. She did it again, and pointed down the road, and then he understood.

The runners would come back; they would drink. They would throw their cups. Messy, messy! She gave him a cardboard box, so he understood, even before she took a felt pen and wrote "For Dirty Cups" on it.

Okay. He grinned. The old ladies and men smiled at him and patted his head. He saw Marti say, ". . . deaf . . ."

He stood by the tables with his box for awhile, and then Marti came and got him, put his box under a table, and set him up on the hood of a truck. Colored flags were shaking all around. People ran and lined up outside the flags. It looked like a carnival, or a little street, but no cars. The runners would run like cars.

He was up high, so he could see over heads. By the long, white ribbon-line arms waved and babies got up on shoulders of people. Everyone looked down the road, and then two men came running.

People with big cameras leaned over.

The men had fast legs and no shirts and hair flying, and they didn't look at each other. They ran with angry-faces, and people clapped. Nicky clapped til his hands hurt. They came closer and closer, and then one bent forward and ran right into the white ribbon. It stretched til it broke. People clapped and flapped, and the men leaned back and slowed down and hugged each other, like love. And then there were more coming, real quick. Marti was writing and writing, and people had clocks in their hands.

Nicky slid down off the truck and ran to the table for his box. Runners dripped water like showers, and bending down, blew on him, puff, puff. They held sticks in their hands like doctors push down your throat, with numbers, and when old ladies got sticks, they gave T-shirts. Sticks were play-money. He saw them get cups and drink, and some poured water over their heads, too, which made him laugh, but Joel said they'd do that. Mouths all came wide open, ha ha ha, and some sat down. Cups fell on the ground, and Nicky ran around between legs and got them. He put cups inside cups in a stack in his box. Maybe they'd need them again; Marti didn't say.

He looked for Joel, when the cups didn't fall so fast, and a man took his box to a trash can. Nicky got busy and filled it up again. This was fun. Some didn't want to give up their cups, and pushed him away when he grabbed for them. Some went and got more water. A lady gave him a drink, but it wasn't water; it tasted like weak lemonade. Coming out of green garbage cans. That was funny. Leah and Elyse would laugh to hear about lemonade in garbage cans!

Now more ladies came running, and they were wet, too. Men hugged them. Little boys ran, but no little tiny girl. He made one old man show him his watch, and it was almost one o'clock. He wasn't hungry, though.

A big boy smiled and gave Nicky a push—a nice, helping push—so Nicky ran toward the table with trophies and climbed in the back of a pickup. He watched a man waving people come, come, come. It was like Christmas, now, with presents for wet people, but most were dry now. Old men got statues, and young men, and ladies. Also a boy like him. People clapped, and he clapped hard, too. He liked to clap, like at plays when they stop acting.

Where was Joel? No prize for Joel. Joel once said to him, "Frank gets prizes. Frank gives speeches. Frank is famous, and I am not."

Frank was Joel's deaf brother.

When all the prizes were gone but one, he found Marti, and she was working, carrying more papers. He asked where Joel was very clearly, and she pointed up the road and didn't look happy. A big man with yellow hair was following her everywhere. Nicky saw him hug her, and didn't like that.

Old ladies came running now, with white hair, and old men, and some young men, limping. They didn't get trophies.

Later on, someone grabbed him from behind, and it was Marti. She had a bike, a boy's bike, and she motioned him to get up on the bar in front of her. He did and held onto the handlebars. She went fast up the road. It was funny to ride toward people coming the other way, not running very good. They all had numbers on; one was upside down. A man was lying by the road, so Marti put on the brakes. Then he smiled and sat up. Nicky saw lots of cups on the road and wondered if he needed to pick them up, but Marti kept going. Then there were more tables, and girls with green garbage cans. A sign said, "2 MILES."

Marti pedalled hard, because it was uphill. She went pant, pant, pant, on the back of his neck. He wished he could help, but he couldn't reach the pedals.

An ambulance went by with flashing light, waving, and they waved back. No one was in it. People with clocks in hands stood by the road. Some people were sitting down, holding legs. Or taking off shoes.

Then Marti hit brakes so hard that Nicky fell across the handlebars and went "Yuk!"

He saw the red clothes and the big mama and the little girl with yellow hair. Joel was here, but at first Nicky didn't know him; his hair hung down on his face, wet. He had his shirt tied around him, and he was looking mad at the red lady.

Marti turned the bike around fast and followed them. The little girl, Nicky saw, was crying. She wasn't running, she was dragging from Mama, and her knees were scraped. His knees hurt too, seeing blood all gishy. Then Joel grabbed Redlady by the arm and pulled, so she stopped, and her mouth went open and shut, real mad. Joel picked up the little girl and ran toward them.

Marti dropped Nicky off the bike, and Joel put the little girl on the bike where Nicky had sat. When Red-lady came, Joel pulled her back. Marti started pedaling, Joel grabbed Nicky's hand, and they ran fast as they could behind Marti's bike. Red-lady couldn't keep up.

When Red-lady was far behind them, Marti stopped, and Joel put the little baby girl on his shoulders, holding her feet, and she pulled his hair. She wasn't crying anymore.

Nicky wanted to run, but Joel said, "Ride bike," so he got on with Marti again. They went back fast to the flag-road, coasting a lot.

When Joel came running, he looked funny with yellow hair on the little girl on top of him. People clapped and clapped and looked at watches. It was 2:50. Afternoon.

When a man came with a bag, Nicky knew he was a doctor. He washed the little girl's knees and put on medicine. Marti came next, with a trophy, and gave it to the little girl. Everyone clapped. Later, Red-lady came running, but she had to stop and throw up. Then she sat down. Nicky brought little girl a cup of garbage-can lemonade, and she had a T-shirt with "Pine Mountain Marathon" that covered up her legs. Men took her picture and made him get in one picture, hugging her like little sister, and he made a funny face at the camera.

Then Joel got Nicky by the hand, and they walked to the camper. Nicky asked could he join races someday.

Joel said, "Sure."

"Is Marti happy?" Nicky asked, and Joel said yes.

Nicky didn't have to ask was Red-lady happy. He knew she wasn't at all.

Marti

"I'll give you a hand so we can clear out of here, tonight," Joel muttered. "But I can't help you shed the Incredible Hulk."

Mike Curran, tall and blond, wore sweatpants, a size XL Pine Mountain Marathon T-shirt, and a friendly grin.

"How about a little post-race party?" he inquired. "I'd ask 'Your place or mine?' but my Volvo isn't exactly the roomiest—"

"I've got a heavy schedule tonight, Mike," she said.

How she'd once appreciated having him around when other runners had sped off in cars with wives and kids, leaving her behind with cleanup crews and tabulation of results for the newspapers. Post-partum depression.

"A guy and a kid, both? Fast work!" Mike said bleakly.

(Her eyes told him that much? Around Nicky, you learn to talk with more than your mouth.)

"What'd you run?" Joel asked, strolling over, looking up at the ex-footballer, who kept his hand on the small of Marti's back. "A two-thirty?"

"Three-twenty."

You couldn't say Mike wasn't honest. Unlike Joel.

"Let's go, Marti," Joel said. "Time's a-wasting."

It was dusk, and her crew had watched themselves on TV in a house near the finish line. Good coverage. The papers should do as well. Jock would be on page one, she hoped, frozen at the moment of the breaking of the tape, setting the course-record of 2:18:43.

Joel's casual but commanding baritone reached her again.

"Nicky's famished, and we want to be in Pennsylvania tomorrow morning, remember."

That did it. Tomorrow morning. Okay! Goodbye Mike. Nice knowing you. See you at the Kapland Marathon in November. Nice flat Ohio course and a fast field. Better luck then.

She said something like that, and then Joel led her away, lugging boxes on each of his shoulders. Nicky carried her bullhorn.

"I cannot trust you!" she hissed, the moment Mike was behind them. "You never hinted you weren't going near Pittsburgh!"

Joel couldn't sign with both arms full, so he didn't answer.

"Talk to me!" she demanded. "Did you even once telephone his father? Or Nicky's brother and sisters?"

"I got Nicky over a suicide-attempt," he said.

Hopeless. She had to leave them in the camper, go to the McCoys' place for her dog and her stuff, thank everyone, and collect her little check. She first retrieved her car-keys and pocketed them. No doubt Joel had made himself an extra set.

After they'd driven past the newspaper office, they ate hamburgers at a drive-in, and listened to Nicky's excited description of the race. It was too late by then to drive very far north. She drooped. "I'll drive," Joel offered.

"Where?" she asked, almost venomously.

"Since you're so eager to reach Pittsburgh, you and Nicky go back in the camper and sleep while I drive. I only jogged it. I'm okay."

"You lugged a child for the last three miles."

He leaned back in the seat and whistled. "Wasn't that something? I haven't heard language like hers since the Navy. Bitch of a child-exploiter. A divorcee. Bet her only buddy is that poor little kid."

"You chatted that much with her?"

"For the first twelve miles. She wasn't in any shape for a marathon. The kid did better than she for the first half. By the way, thanks for keeping an extra trophy for the kid. She earned it merely by surviving."

"Was the little girl hurt, more than her knees?"

"Not physically, I don't think so. But I'll bet she'll always hate running. Probably hate Mommy, too. For good reason."

"We must call Mr. Strathgordon in Knoxville," Marti said abruptly. "Call from some gas station. The police may be after us. Think about poor Annalee, and Alan Teague, and—"

"Who?"

"Nicky's speech teacher. Alan Teague. Do you know him, after all?"

"TEAGUE?" he almost shouted. "The imitation hearie? That louse was Nicky's TEACHER?"

"He talks."

Joel let out a vivid oath, making Marti stiffen in the neon glow of the Burger-Boy sign. Nicky sat in a corner of the front seat, solemnly watching Joel's hands.

"Alan talks because his mother drilled him and drilled him," she said.

"I'll say she did. Like with a gun. I've known Alan for years. The fraud!"

"You mean he isn't really DEAF? Oh, come ON!"

Joel's signs began to look like prizefighter's punches, as he alternated messages to Nicky and words to Marti. "He has a terrific voice, and he's a fantastic speechreader, Marti. They're almost impossible skills. But Alan was deafened at four by meningitis. He was not born deaf."

"SO? Deaf at birth or four, is there much difference?"

"The difference between . . . between . . ." his hands flew sideways to encompass the interior of the cab. "Between blindness and sight, Marti. Between life and death! Alan heard speech and learned the structure of English for four whole years. He heard his own voice. Look," he closed his eyes for a minute as if he were counting to ten. "Look, a hearing kid of five, they calculate, speaks about two thousand words, and understands about 25,000. Twenty-five THOUSAND, I said. Most born-deaf kids at five speak a dozen words and speechread a hundred. That is not language. Not communication. You can't ask a question or get any answer with that pittance."

"But Nicky—"

"Can you imagine Nicky, at nine, not having been able to ask one question in his whole life? That happens all the time. He might as well be retarded; he'd seem like it."

"But Alan—"

"Marti," he said, "make your tongue lie completely limp in your mouth."

"I can't."

"Try."

She found that she could.

"Now talk with everything else working right—lips, teeth, larynx."

She tried it, over and over. She sounded like Nicky. No, much worse.

"See? Tongue-control's a major key. And how can he see people's tongues, inside their mouths, to imitate them?"

"Don't any of the born-deaf talk?"

"They've got a rough estimate. Four percent, maybe five percent get fluent voices. I worry about the other ninety-five."

"You're depressing me terribly."

"But it's not hopeless. The thing is, Marti," he said, leaning closer to her, vibrating with enthusiasm, "Once they've got language—the pattern of any language, American Sign Language, English, French—they can work on better speech any time. Even as adults. But people don't absorb a first language after age five or six. The brain doesn't wait around. It's early, or never. And English is the hardest language on the face of the globe, the most unpredictable, unpronounceable, with the largest vocabulary. I've seen what happens. Take my dad. He knows far less than Nicky already does, and he's sixty-four! An almost-illiterate chess-champ. Mom started him on his first language—ASL—when he was fourteen!"

"How about your mom?" Dizzy, she felt intensely curious.

"Mom's educated, reads all the time, talks and speechreads. A pretty cool old lady. Fourth-generation deaf."

"I wish someone told me this sooner."

Joel's pouchy eyes were intent on her face; his hair had dried into curls. "Alan's keeping most of the voice he had at four is lucky for him and damned useful, but the deaf kids today are being born deaf. Mostly German-measles kids with hearing parents plus multiple disabilities—poor sight, poor hearts, hyperactivity, aphasia. Oralism, ninety-five cases out of a hundred, cheats them of everything they could have. No language develops, even to think with. Amplify, work on speech, if you must, but sign, sign, sign!"

"You don't like Alan Teague?" she asked.

"He's the laughing-stock of the deaf community. His mother said she loved him, but made sure he'd never even meet anyone else like him. How are deaf people supposed to speech-read Alan, with his pronunciation? He won't date deaf women. Not even Miss Deaf America with a college degree and a voice, because she signs. His few oral deaf friends all live out of state. He's the loneliest man I ever met, full of pride that masks self-hate. End of lecture."

"I did find that evening rather taxing," she admitted.

"Severe stutterers are not popular, either, and they can hear."

He still was not finished. "Alan runs a computer. Dad was a yard-man all his life, nothing more. But my mom worked her way up to head of a pathology lab. She supported us, really."

He added, "Can you picture a blind man snubbing all other blind people and going around poisoning Seeing-Eye dogs and breaking canes? To make blindness 'invisible'? That's our Alan."

Joel certainly was a master of analogy. She wondered what a psychiatrist would say about his rage.

"Nicky has repressed the hanging incident," he said, ceasing to sign, as Nicky began to drowse in Marti's lap. "He thinks he left with me when Strathgordon kicked me out."

"That's scary. No recollection at ALL?"

"Nope. And the only therapy I can think of is to give him what he most wants."

"What?"

"Easy communication."

"Hasn't he got that, right now? With you?"

"He ought to meet my folks. Talk about Mom, you ought to see my brother. Frank's voice isn't usable, but he's made a life you wouldn't believe. A beautiful wife, kids, two college degrees, and he flies all over the world to education conferences. Makes a pile of money, too."

"Deaf?"

"Sure. The fifth generation. Nine years older'n me." He meditated a moment, then murmured, "But from the time I was two, til Frank went off to college, I was his interpreter."

Marti woke up in a motionless, sunny, warm camper with Nicky sitting up, dangling a chain of safety pins just above her mouth. No Joel. No dog. She snapped like a fish at the chain, making him grin.

"Devil! Little rascal! Where's Joel?" She'd fallen asleep up here with Joel driving, last night. When had he stopped?

She rubbed breath-mist off the forward window and stared. They weren't parked in a highway rest-area, as she'd expected, but in some city's residential section. Small frame houses, close together, pocket-size lawns . . . but where? Pittsburgh? House numbers and street signs don't give a clue to their city.

Joel wasn't anywhere in sight. No store where he might buy breakfast-makings, or a cafe to have coffee. So?

"Hey, what's with Joel?" she asked, and wrote on Nicky's ever-ready pad, "Did you see Joel leave? Where are we?" A shrug and a shaken head.

Maybe Nicky knew, maybe he didn't. Joel was capable of teaching him deceit.

When she reached for her shoes, she found one foot did not penetrate past a folded piece of paper.

"I'm at 1740," it said. "Hope you enjoyed your sleep. I needed a bath, and you can bathe and eat here." It was, of course, signed "Joel."

"Great!" she cried, suddenly aware how grungy she felt, after sleeping in her clothes. But was this Pittsburgh? It couldn't be Nicky's house, or he would have told her; right? Joel likely had contacts all along their route. This darned sight better be Pennsylvania!

She led Nicky out of the camper, and up to number 1740.

The small white house peered through creepers like a just-awakened sleeper through uncombed hair. Hydrangeas, blue and purple balls, bordered the front porch. Marti marched up the steps and rang the doorbell.

While they waited, Nicky pointed to the door and put a thumb on his cheek with his hand open. She'd seen that sign. What was it? Man? No, Mama. Mother. MOTHER?

Then it hit her. Where Joel would take them, though heaven knows to what city in what state. She almost turned and fled, before she sensed the vibration of someone approaching the door.

"Into the freak-show tent?" she thought frantically, embarrassed.

What will these people LOOK like? Do? Wear? Think?

"Oh, please God, let me behave right."

The door swung open (who'd heard the doorbell ring?), and a stocky little woman in pink stood smiling. Across the room, a short, balding man turned to face her. Hildie lay on the rug, also smiling, thumping her tail at Marti.

The woman, heavily corseted under a linen dress, had Joel's pouchy, sad eyes in a much happier face. Nicky bumped Marti aside; his hands flew. He did not speak or move his lips, but his eyes danced.

The old man came forward—straight out of a Norman Rockwell painting—high-waisted, in suspenders and house-slippers.

"Mrs. . . . Dalton?" Marti faltered, and the lady said "Yes? Mahtie?" She put out her hand and drew Marti inside, eyeing Nicky all the while. Marti yearned to know what Nicky was saying to them, continuously and impishly pointing.

"I'm . . . Marti Hanson. Looking for Joel. Your son is Joel?"

"Yes, I know," she murmured, nodding. "Ee tol' meh." (Pointing down) HE told her; Nicky did.

The old man stuck out a hand, and Marti shook it. He produced a few flowing gestures, watching her face for comprehension. Then he dropped his gaze to Nicky. Nicky struck his forehead, which Marti recognized. Stupid, yes. "Stupid me," she signed, and got a sudden maternal hug. The man's face glowed. "Sorry," she shook her head. "I don't understand signs. Yet."

Joel's father came closer, flicking his finger up off his forehead, mouthing the word "understand." He shook his head. "Don't understand."

(So easy as that?)

She held up the I-love-you, and both of them, in unison, let out sighs of gratification. Mrs. Dalton kissed her.

"Please, where am I?" Marti asked, holding out her hands, palm-up, beseechingly.

"De Dawton haas," replied Mrs. Dalton in her pleasant sing-song. "Wahl-come, Mahtie."

"What city?" Marti asked, but that would not be clear, even were they staring into her mouth. Mrs. Dalton said, "Oo ate backfust heyah." Marti was catching on. They'd eat breakfast here. So Joel said.

"Where is Joel?"

"Baath . . . soon . . ." she replied; Joel's father cheerfully scrubbed his chest and toweled his back. He certainly had no inhibitions, no self-effacing mannerisms. He patted his stomach and flipped a hand up under his chin, then pointed to Nicky and to her and vigorously spooned phantom food into his mouth.

Their livingroom was decorated in reds and oranges; the sun blasted through dimity curtains. Plastic flowers and real fruit decorated the coffee table, and real flowers and wax fruit the old-fashioned sideboard. The room was full of overstuffed furniture, knick-knack shelves, and potted ferns. Framed photographs lined the bookcase and looked down from all the walls. She'd never seen so many pictures per square foot of room-space, before.

In the dining-area stood a small yellow table. Chairs were jerked out for them; they sat down. Like a Mom and Pop cafe, but the restaurant-owner in the house probably drowned in his bath. Weird. She could raise her voice to shout, "Joel! Where am I?" and not one of these three would know it. But manners are manners, regardless of what you can get away with.

"Cocoa? Like cocoa?"

"Yes!"

(She remembered Joel's crack about deaf people asking for beer and getting milk. Until he demonstrated, she couldn't believe such words lipread identically.)

"Where are we?" she tried on Joel's father, who sat down beside her, smiling all over his rather Scottish face.

Nicky shoved his notepad at Marti, but the man frowned. He made rapid signs to Nicky. When Marti scribbled, "What city is this?" it was Nicky who took the pad, read it, and signed to Mr. Dalton.

Marti, wide-eyed, shot a glance at Joel's mother, but she was busy over the frying pan.

Instantly a message flew across the table, lots of finger-action, and Nicky slowly inscribed, "Front Royal."

"Huh?"

Marti leaned sideways, touched Mrs. Dalton's apron-bow, and showed her the notepad.

"Fun Oil, yes!" she smiled, nodding.

"In what state?" She was losing her appetite. Had Joel the gall to drive south, not north? Had he dared take them far off the route to Pittsburgh? She pictured herself shoving Joel's head under water and holding it down til the bubbles ceased. WHERE ARE WE?

Plates of scrambled eggs and bacon were set before them.

"In what state?" she wrote to Nicky, who put down his spoon to sign, watch Joel's father, and then write, "VA."

Virginia! Not Georgia or Florida, thank God, but Virginia was a heckuva long state. This was ridiculous. Twenty Questions. With all her driving, she'd never gone through any Front Royal. She had the feeling "Royal" townships would tend to cluster on the eastern seaboard. Nearest England. (Joel, I am going to kill you. Slowly.)

Mrs. Dalton brought the cocoa and sat herself down opposite Marti. "My family deaf, all deaf—back and back and back," she said, her hands circling each other up and over her shoulder. "Grandmothers, grandfathers, all."

Marti nodded. She was busy forking eggs, but she drew a rough map of Virginia on Nicky's pad. Like a shoe, pointing west. She didn't get a chance to pass it to Mrs. Dalton, because Mr. Dalton grabbed it, grinning. He took the pencil and wrote "Wash, D.C."—with a circle. Then he made an X to the left of that, but not far left. Marti, unheard, said, "Damn!"

"Pittsburgh," she scribbled; he frowned, and Nicky touched fingertips to his chest. The old man nodded. "Ahh."

He added a square, inscribed it "W. VA.," and located Pittsburgh above that state. There. He added Ohio, Ken., and Tenn., indicated Knoxville with a K, said "Joel," very understandably, and passed her the butter for her toast.

There was nothing to do now but eat, and that was a pleasure. Nicky finished quickly, and was carrying on an animated dialogue. She wondered if Joel had told anyone about the suicide-attempt. Joel's mother touched her arm, pointed to her husband and said, "Grandpa! Two grandchildren. A boy and a girl. So pretty, so sweet. Like Nicky."

And then, "You like Joel?"

Everyone waited for her answer, six eyes glowing.

She might've said, "I could happily murder him, right now. He's infuriating." Instead, she had a brainstorm: she made the I-love-you handshape and flipped it, thumb-down.

Eyebrows rose. That communicated.

"We must leave," she explained, driving an invisible car. "Now. Where is Joel?"

"No!" said Nicky, glowering.

Mrs. Dalton sprang up and ran to look down the hall, returning with the news that Joel was now taking a nap (folding her hands under her cheek; closing her eyes) "Tired. He must be very tired. Such a long, long drive!"

Long? You bet it was. Not due-north to Pittsburgh, but northeast—almost to Washington, D.C.

Marti went past her down the hall and reached for the first doorknob. The woman stopped her.

"No! No clothes on!" she cried in consternation almost comical.

"You wake him up, then!"

"Joel is tired!"

Marti groaned. That concerned, compassionate maternal face would stop an army on the march. Joel's mother patted her, soothed her, led her back into the livingroom, and took her on a tour of the photo gallery.

Mr. Dalton joined them, drawing Marti's hand through his arm, teasingly cocking his head. She had no trouble understanding. Frank and Joel as fat babies, Joel running—a finish-line shot. Wedding photos, dozens of them, in color, of handsome Frank and his gorgeous, beaming bride. Joel was not the best man. Marti wondered how many of the party were deaf. The attendants, the minister? She pointed to her ears and then at the people.

"Deaf," said Mr. Dalton clearly, and picked them out:

Best man, flower-girl, bride, brides-maids, parents of the groom. Parents of the bride? No. "No, no," he said, making a sad face. Marti squinted at the picture, imagining she saw anxious embarrassment on the faces of the couple whose deaf daughter was marrying a deaf Dalton. Then there was Joel, surprising in a gray suit, on the fringes of the reception crowd.

Curiosity made Marti point again to the bride's beautifully dressed parents. "They sign?" she asked, moving her hands.

Both heads shook. "No. Never. Very sad," said Mrs. Dalton.

Her husband signed something toward Nicky, who took out his trusty pad and diligently wrote, "Peg is our daughter now. She is like you. You are wonderful. Please stay with us, tonight."

All that?

Marti shook her head, no. Carefully, she said, "We must get Nicky home to his mother."

"No!" Nicky said. "I stay here!" Loudly and clearly.

Marti felt a flush flag her cheeks.

"See grandchildren," said Grandmother blithely, as she drew Marti further along the wall.

Marti suddenly asked, "How old is Joel?"

His father held up index finger and thumb, then made them into a circle and raised the other three fingers. Did they think she was THAT smart? Then he shook his head, smiled apologetically, and flashed two hands at her, fingers spread, then two more, then five fingers and four. Twenty-nine?

He nodded.

Funny, here she was wondering if Frank had a hearie wife, and she didn't even know if Joel was married. Or ever had been. She knew next to nothing about him.

"Is Joel married?" she mouthed at Mrs. Dalton.

His parents beamed, glanced at each other. The answer was an emphatic no. Marti turned to a table with the DEAF AMERICAN lying on top of TIME magazine, picked it up and flipped through it, and when she looked around again, her hosts had dispersed. Nicky and Mr. Dalton came back lugging between them a tall aluminum ladder, which they erected in the hallway. Nicky scrambled up it and helped the man bring down through the ceiling trap-door a big box.

Marti had no chance to see them open it. Joel's mother was tugging her into a bedroom where she opened a drawer full of quilt covers, dozens of them in squares and solids and prints, metallic fabrics and brocades, sun-bursts, wheels, and circles in every shade of color. Marti held her cheeks in astonishment. "Do you make all these? Sell them?" she asked, rubbing fingers on thumb to mean money. She wanted one. Her bedspread was monkscloth and horrid.

"Sell, no. Give, yes. Give to you. Pick one."

Marti shook her head. "I couldn't. They'd cost a fortune in a store."

That did not communicate, but her face did. "Pick; choose!" the little woman commanded, spreading quilt-covers on both beds. Affection as hard to shove aside as a warm coat on a cold day. Marti liked them. She wanted to hug them, as if they were hers. She didn't see enough of her parents, and they were a huggy trio. Like this.

She had to choose a quilt—one in autumn colors that reminded her of the Smokies in October. Her choice was bundled up and tucked under her arm, the seamstress treating it too roughly for comfort. She kissed the little woman, and got a rib-busting hug in return and comments she didn't understand in the rush of breathy vowels.

In the livingroom, Mr. Dalton and Nicky were down on their knees with figure-8's of track around them, feverishly covering the rug. Mrs. Dalton stamped her foot for attention and unmistakably requested that paths be left for large pedestrians. A little village was going up, cardboard houses in bright colors snapped into cubes with tabs and slits.

"Frankes," Mr. Dalton muttered. "Baby Frankes, baby Joeles." Her young interpreter was busy playing engineer.

Mama Dalton handed Marti a slip of paper with explicit directions what to buy to complete the quilt, and how to sew the parts together. "You sew?" "I sew." Big smile.

Nicky clapped his hands in delight as the tiny buzzing engine pulled its brown, red, and yellow cars faster and faster around curves, through a tunnel, and under the furniture, making the little houses wobble with the breeze it made.

Only then did Joel finally appear, scuffling across the braided rug in stocking-feet, his jeans sagging off his hips, his shirt-tail out. He'd shaved, and combed his hair. He yawned. Completely at home.

"How're you getting along, Marti?"

"Be great if *I* could forget all about Nicky's problems," she began, a mile a minute. "If *I* didn't have to worry about getting Nicky home, and avoiding the commission of a felony! It took me half an hour to find out where we ARE, and– Hey, don't sign!"

Stubbornly, his hands kept flying.

"Your folks are darling, but we must—"

He said, "Nicky sure looks happy."

"How much have you told . . . everybody?"

"Everything. That was quite a drive, straight through, after a marathon, slow as I jogged it. I needed the nap."

"We are just west of Washington, D.C., Joel. Your father told me."

"He told you, huh?" Joel grinned at his father. "Good job, Pop. Pretty smart, isn't she?"

"Do you want your folks hauled in for sheltering a runaway? A pair of kidnappers, Joel?"

He didn't sign those words, she noticed.

"Okay. We'll head out tomorrow morning. Stay the night here. I haven't seen them in a month. What's for lunch, Mom?" He teasingly tapped his little mother on her corset.

"They practically have me in the family, and Nicky, too. Don't they REALIZE—"

"Realize what?"

"Oh, shit, Joel!"

"There's a sign for that, remember."

"You don't have to sign it."

"You don't have to say it!"

She sank down in a chair and covered her eyes with spread fingers. "I want my car-keys back," she muttered in the silent room where everyone was talking at once. No one could see her lips move.

Joel pretended he didn't hear her.

Joel

"Yeah, I called Knoxville again," Joel admitted. "Not today; back on Thursday or on Friday."

(It was Sunday; his folks would be in church if he hadn't arrived and kept them home.)

"You said you didn't! You liar!" said Marti.

"I didn't say I never called, just that Nicky's dad didn't deserve it."

Marti was so insistent that for fear she'd run out in search of a phone, or discover that his folks owned one, he admitted the truth.

Yes, he should have told her before, but face it, he didn't want to think about that telephone conversation.

He'd again reached Strathgordon's wife, Annalee. Strathgordon was at work. He didn't tell Marti that Annalee talked and talked and talked to him.

"I just said Nicky was fine; that he'd be in Pittsburgh in a few days, once I was sure his Mom had gotten home."

That didn't seem to content her. "What did Annalee say?" asked Marti, and he responded, "Nothing much."

What he didn't describe was the woman's going on and on about wanting a kid so badly, any age, to complete her husband's life and hold her marriage together. She wanted to keep her husband. She "adored" him.

Joel wondered if at eleven in the morning she'd been drinking. He didn't want to listen, but it wasn't in him to hang up on her. Lanier was terribly upset. The police were not.

It didn't matter to her, Annalee moaned, if Nicky talked. She'd study sign language. Make Lanier learn it, too. Just so Nicky was all right. She'd make his father treat him right. Lanier must have custody of Nicky. Don't tell the people in Pittsburgh that Nicky . . . that Nicky (Joel had waited, wincing, for her to say the words) that "he tried to hurt himself." Don't tell his mother and his brother and sisters, please.

"You still aren't getting him back," Joel had said. "His father had his chance."

Pretty mild words, but she was crying into the phone.

He suggested that she give Lanier a child.

How could he advise her? What business did he have talking to the wife of a man who hated his guts? He got off the phone after forty minutes, feeling wilted and blue. He had to remind himself of the looped curtain-cord Marti brought along with her, in order to build up his anger against Strathgordon again.

Marti summoned him out on the side porch the minute Mom rushed away to cook lunch, and Dad went out to attempt Frisbee with Nicky in the back yard. Marti's dog did a better job of catching the Frisbee than Dad did.

Admittedly he'd rattled on too long and too bluntly about the hit she made with his parents. Then he'd interpreted compliments dripping with affection. She was still pouting, when he asked didn't she see how Nicky prospered, here? She came right back at him about "Nicky's poor, poor mother."

"To HELL with Nicky's mother!" he'd said, which really teed her off. Now she had him alone, she was really sticking in the knives and twisting them.

"Can't anybody else on earth be fair to deaf people, but you?" she shot at him. "Must you lord it over everyone?"

He didn't have time to describe prejudice and scorn, tell her how many friends were scared stiff to meet his folks. She really rocked him.

"Saint Joel! If everyone else acts rotten, that makes you the only good person. Isn't that it?" She turned her face away from him.

She wasn't shrill, wasn't screeching; her voice went down in volume, so he had to strain to hear her.

"You make me sick," she whispered. "Knight on a white charger! Nicky's holy savior. I begin to see where you get your kicks, Joel. From congratulating yourself!"

And here he'd begun to picture himself someday proposing marriage to her! He'd had hopes from the first time she produced, without knowing it, some lovely nonverbal communication. She was the first hearie to make his folks say, "She's the right one for you."

"For us," they also meant. But Marti was calling him names that hurt so much he couldn't look at her.

"I'm disappointed in you," she continued. "Okay, Nicky's father is a jerk. I'll buy that. Alan's something of a creep, too. But to insult Nicky's mother, sight-unseen—"

"Okay. Maybe she's great. But Nicky doesn't want her."

"Tough," she said, with a bleak face. "He's got to go home. Why'd you drag him off where he'd want to stay? That's the second disservice you've done him."

"What's the other?" he demanded.

"You left Nicky that last night at his father's without one word of reassurance, without really cautioning me how bad off he was."

Joel blinked. Winced. "Maybe," he blurted. "Who knows motives? For coming here, maybe I had another reason, too. I wanted my folks to meet you."

"Gee, thanks!"

"You do like them, don't you?"

"That's irrelevant!" she hissed, hugging herself, leaning against a porch column and frowning at the floor. Then she relented. "Don't get me wrong. They're darling. They're sweet, and obviously they're smart, and they enjoy life, like you said. But this was not the time, Joel. We are supposed to be in Pittsburgh."

"You wouldn't have come over here after Pittsburgh."

"Darned right! I'm due in Indianapolis to see my own family."

"It's only Sunday still."

She seemed surprised. He felt surprised, too. He'd been the one awake all night to drive the 450 miles from Pine Mountain.

"Can I say I'm sorry?"

"I'll bet you are!"

"Saint Joel is apologizing, so listen!" he forced himself to say, hating his croaking voice. "Maybe you've got a point."

He wanted to say, "Don't blame a man in love," but in lieu of saying that, he couldn't say anything.

"Do other kids of deaf parents act like you?"

Jolt.

He ventured to give a worthy example. "No one seems yet to know 'deaf-mute' and 'deaf-and-dumb' are as insulting as 'nigger.' Someone's got to tell them."

"Well, I'll start telling them, too. But look how you overshoot. Overkill. Make enemies."

He wanted to put his arms around her. The urge was centered up in his heart, but soon he'd feel it all over. Marti broke his heart. She'd always been straight with him. SHE'd never lied.

He felt like a drink. A tranquilizer. Cocktails before dinner. In this teetotalling house? Leave Nicky to entertain the folks and take Marti to a show, he told himself, knowing she'd never agree. Take her for a ride. In her camper. No, in the folks' car. Show her the view off Skyline Drive. Did she suspect she was on a mountain near gorgeous forested cliffs? Take her out to dinner? He cast about for something appealing to offer, but "Let's take a run, together" made him ache. He was still too stiff and sore. Hopeless.

But Marti was still there on the porch with him, and not because she dreaded the other people in this house. He'd seen her, relaxed, trading visual jokes with his dad, listening intently to his mother's skewed pronunciation that took most strangers a week to catch onto. Sure, they already had him married to her and were counting their grandchildren. He wouldn't mind that. She was pure gold. Why was she running around single, prey to Incredible Hulks who raced slower than he did, on a good day?

Because she loved her work, that's why. He groaned to himself. Traveling salesmen, cross-country truck-drivers, airline pilots—fine work for a man, not for any man's wife? She'd never give up traveling for him; and for a bunch of deafies.

He'd said it. Not aloud, just to himself. "Deafies." Closed his eyes and felt the sick sensation rise. God, he hated that term, though many deaf people used it among themselves, the way blacks say, "You crazy nigger!"

"What we've got to think about now," Marti said solemnly, "to the exclusion of everything else, is how to get Nicky home and happy. Happy at home, I mean, where he belongs."

He nodded, still finding it impossible to meet her gaze.

She touched the back of his dangling hand, and his hand grabbed hers before he told it to.

"Tomorrow at dawn, okay?" she said. "We leave then. And I want my car keys back. Right now."

He handed them over to her. Out of his jeans pocket into hers.

Nicky

"I am going to live with you forever," Nicky said.

Joel's Daddy missed the Frisbee again, so Hildie got it and brought it back. His slippers kept slipping off in the grass, and Joel's mama in the window signed, "Put on shoes."

So Grandpa went in and did. Shoes for grass. Nicky signed "Sit," and Hildie-dog did.

The marathon was fun, but this was funner. Joel's mama and daddy told him things, and asked about home and Kirby and Leah and Elyse, and said they were smart for hearies.

"When did you start Sign?" they asked, and he remembered what Joel said. He said the same: "I was born signing."

Behind their house, down a path, Grandpa showed him a little creek, and a nice place under tree-roots like a cave. Nicky could hide there if Joel and Marti tried to make him leave.

He was the happiest here since the night Joel saved him. From Daddy's big, bloody axe.

The train was fun. He put houses on the track, and the train knocked them down, and then Joel picked him up, upside down, and tickled him, til he yelled and laughed. He was so full of food that Grandpa said he'd get fat, like Santa Claus, and that reminded him what Joel said about Marti.

When they got here, early morning, Joel looked in the camper window and signed to him to come out. Marti didn't wake up when he got out of bed. So they went into this house for hugs, and Joel wrote a note and said go put it in Marti's shoe. Marti won't walk barefoot.

Nicky asked why Marti slept late. Joel drove all night, so why did Marti sleep? SHE wasn't tired. Joel said Marti didn't sleep for nights before her marathon, because that was like her Christmas. You don't sleep the night before Santa, do you? Nicky understood.

He went out and very quietly put the note in Marti's shoe saying where they were. In house. He came back, and ate and talked, and then Joel looked at clock and said, "Go wake Marti.

"I take bath. You get Marti."

That was fun. He went in the camper again very quiet, and she was sleeping on her back with her mouth a little open like for "T." Maybe she was snoring. He found a box with race things, and a chain made out of safety pins. She looked like a big fish, so he took the chain and opened the last pin like a hook. He went up to the bed very quiet. He was going to catch her like a fish, in the lip, and then he thought that might hurt her. So he shut the last safety pin like the others, and tried to see if he could slide chain in her mouth, like kids' braces on teeth, before she woke. But it looked so funny he laughed, and she heard him and opened her eyes and shut her mouth, bite, bite. Then she hugged and kissed him, and then she got worried.

Then she was scared of the house, and then she was happy with Grandma and Grandpa. When Joel came she was mad again. No wonder she got tired and had to sleep a lot.

Grandpa Dalton stopped Frisbee and asked how did Joel save him. "Tell, tell, again."

Nicky told about holding onto Joel, and wicked, mean Daddy pulled him away, and he screamed and hit, hit, hit, so Joel hit Daddy in the face. Joel hit, like on TV, bam, bam, bam, all the bad people. They fell down, and Joel grabbed his hand, and they ran out the door, fast, and Marti ran, too, and they got in the truck, and Joel drove fast, fast.

"Hurt you?" Grandpa asked, and Nicky said, "Tried to cut my head off." Grandpa wanted to look at his neck, and Nicky let him. It didn't show because Marti made it go away. With a big, bloody axe they tried to cut his head off, and they were dead because Joel killed them, bang, bang, bang.

But he didn't want to think about it.

In the house, Grandma asked where did they sleep.

He told her about climbing the mountain, and she asked did Joel and Martie sleep in the camper bed? Nicky remembered the first night they did, and told her, and then said, "I slept between." She said "Oh," with a funny face.

Joel was funny here, too. When Nicky first came in the house, Joel said, "Don't use voice," and put his hand over Nicky's mouth. "You aren't a hearie. Be proud to be deaf."

Joel's mama asked why, and Joel said "Be proud." Nicky said he was, and Joel said some deaf weren't, and Nicky said "I can read like a hearie."

Grandpa gave him a magazine, and he opened it and made all the words into signs one after another. Joel said, "That's English, not ASL."

So Nicky did it again, in ASL, translating fast, and they made big eyes and said "Smart, smart!" Nicky was bored with all the big words in the magazine, so he turned to a joke-page and signed a joke. Grandpa laughed, so he knew he did ASL.

Joel said things like "deaf pride" and "birthright," and his mama said, "I think Joel really wants to be deaf, but I want to hear!"

Grandpa said he was too old to hear, if it could happen. Scary. That was funny. Nicky never thought much about that. How hearing would be.

He told them about dumb kids in school that didn't talk to each other. Thinking about school made him miss his. Especially when they said they knew kids there and one teacher. (They knew every deafbody in America, Joel said.)

They kept saying he was lucky. Lucky, lucky Nicky.

Joel talked about honeymoon and Japan and Mama, but Nicky didn't want to watch. He went to look at the rest of the house.

House had two bedrooms and a big bathroom, and he found Joel's wet towel on tub, so like Mama always said always to do, Nicky hung it up on the rack.

Jesus was on the wall, and he found a shelf with trophies, and read them. They said "Joseph Dalton" and "Bowling." One was for Joel, and said "5-Mile Race, First." Pictures, pictures on walls. He never saw so many pictures.

It got all mixed up in his head, there were so many people, and such fun. Marti was a hearie, and needed pad to talk. He wrote for her. She and Grandpa drew maps together, and she looked at baby-pictures, and Grandpa said the train was new for Joel's brother, and then Joel played with it, and Frank's little boy played with it, and someday Joel's little boy would play with it; but Grandma said girls like trains, too, and soon Miriam would be old enough for the train, and also Joel might have a little girl; you never know.

Marti took Joel away, and Grandma was worried, and Grandpa said leave them alone. Nicky could see Marti on the porch with mad-face, and no signs, so he didn't know why mad. Joel was sad, sad. He wondered if she didn't like the note put in her shoe.

At lunch, Marti wanted to know how did Grandpa think? When? When Grandpa lived with hearies and had no language. So Grandpa signed, and Joel talked.

When Grandpa was a boy, he made pictures in his head. (Nicky wished he could do that.) Marti asked who talked to him, and Grandpa looked down and signed, "No one."

People pushed him and shoved and pointed, and his sisters and brothers on the farm didn't play with him. They said he was stupid. In the school, he didn't understand anything, and when he was eight, they found out he was deaf.

"Then you went to deaf school?" Marti asked, leaning forward, and he said no, because it was too far away. They told him to watch mouths and everything would be okay.

He wanted a dog, he said. A baby dog, for his own. He tore pictures of dogs from magazines and gave them to his mama, and finally they got him a puppy. That was a happy time. He told a funny story next. Grandpa thought animals talked. Mouths flap open, so he thought both people and animals talked. He was fourteen, before he knew animals don't talk.

"*I* told him," said Grandma.

("Animals DO talk," Nicky said. "They say bow-wow and moo, wolf and meow.")

"I can't believe this!" said Marti.

"ASL is the only child-taught language," Joel said.

Nicky wasn't sure what that meant. He felt bored, and he was sad because their hearing-ear dog was still at school, learning. "At college," signed Grandpa, and laughed.

After lunch, Nicky said, "Excuse me" and ran out and checked his cave under the tree-roots again. He could dig it deeper. He ought to put food there. When he came back, they were talking about Daddy again, and he looked away, but then he saw Joel say, "deaf man," and his name Joel told him was "Alan Teague."

He asked did Joel go kill that bad man, too? Grandma said killing is bad, bad, bad, and Nicky said, I-don't-care" in one sign. Grandpa said God won't love you if you kill people, so Nicky said, "He HURT me!"

Joel was explaining about church to Marti, with interpreters more than in schools. Boring. So Nicky went in the bedroom and lay on the big bed, by the teletypewriter. He looked at it. He went over and read the yellow paper they rolled out of it, that had words about a "masked ball." He didn't know what kind of ball you put a mask on, or why. It said "pirate" and "queen," and "club." He read the words: "SEE YOU THEN IF NO WORD ABOUT CHANGE QN OKAY QN GA SK"

Then, "GOOD MOM MISS YOU FAST COME SEE OKAY SKSK"

He never understood much of other people's TDDing, just GA and SK for Go Ahead and Stop Keying. They didn't ever tear off their paper. It fell down behind the teletypewriter like a big, flat, yellow snake all coiled up covered with typing.

He sat down and put his hands on the keys, but he couldn't do ten fingers, yet, just two fingers. He looked over at the telephone. He was bored. He wanted to call someone. He picked up the blue TDD book with the names and states and looked for Pittsburgh. He saw names he knew all over the page. Not his name, though, because they were waiting to get a little Portatel. Mama didn't like big, grey, noisy TDD's.

He got up and went and closed the bedroom door, very quiet.

He came back and sat down again with the book. Tennessee. No Strathgordon. He looked down all the names for Knoxville.

"Teague, Alan."

Nicky got mad. He got very, very mad, and he also got an idea, but it scared him. He closed the book, and then he opened it up again. He wasn't in Tennessee. He was in Virginia, now. Front Royal in Virginia. He didn't remember long distance, how you do it. "Out-of-state," said directions.

He figured he could try, and maybe it would work. "It won't bite," Mama used to say, when he was afraid of starting the washing machine or dryer. Phones don't bite.

How far away could hearies hear a TDD go? Big ones shook, like at school, and hearies came running when they made it go without asking. Typewriters make noise, too. Was noise and noise louder or softer than just one noise?

Mama once said,"I can't hear you when Kirby is talking. Don't both talk at once."

So maybe it was softer with two.

He picked up the phone and put the receiver on the TDD, face-down. Then he dialed 0 and then the number. Nothing happened. Then he hung up and dialed one and the little code-number for Tennessee: 615.

Then he took two big breaths and looked up the number again. He dialed it. Seven numbers. And he waited.

The light was on, on the machine. and then he saw it go "Flash."

He should be happy, but he was more scared. "Flash."

"Flash" said ringing. Ringing in Knoxville in Tennessee, 615.

"Flash."

If he got a hearie, it would go flicker, flicker, flicker, for voice, and the machine would just sit there and not know what to do.

He didn't want Joel to come in, or Grandpa or Grandma, and catch him. He touched the phone and almost picked up the receiver quick ("Flash"), before the machine jumped, and said:

"ALAN TEAGUE HERE GOOD EVENING GA"

He stared at it. It worked. It happened. He didn't even have to shut his eyes to see Alan Teague, the crazy deaf man, standing there in front of him. His hands shook when he put them on the machine that was waiting. The machine was ready on the next line, so he didn't even need to push Line-Feed.

His fingers typed, "I HATE YOU BAD BAD BAD MAN I WANT TO KILL YOU DEAD"

He didn't type "GA," because he wanted to make him wait and feel scared. You weren't supposed to answer til "GA" came on the Telecommunication Device for the Deaf.

After awhile the machine by itself went back to the left and rolled the paper up and said, very fast, "WHO IS THIS QN

HOW DO YOU DARE SAY THESE THINGS TO ME QN ARE YOU CRAZY QN GA"

Nicky did Line-Feed himself this time and typed, "YOU ARE CRAZY DEAF MAN JOEL WILL KILL YOU TOO" and then he did "GA" to see if Alan Teague was worried.

"I WILL CALL THE POLICE," it said. "WHERE ARE YOU QN IS THIS NICKY STRATHGORDON QN GA"

"I WILL NEVER TELL YOU YOU WILL DIE DIE DIE YOU TIED ME," Nicky typed, "JOEL HATES YOU

MARTI HATES YOU," but before he could do "GA" or "SK," the machine rolled up paper and said (shake, shake, shake): "YOUR FATHER WANTS YOU WHERE ARE YOU NICKY QN YOUR FATHER WENT TO PITTSBURGH TO FIND YOU ARE YOU IN PITTSBURGH QN"

"I NEVER GO BACK TO PITTSBURGH," Nicky said, scowling at the keys under his fingers and looking up to check what he said. Before he did "GA," the machine ran away from him again.

"WHY DOES MARTI HATE ME QN DO YOU TELL LIES QN GA"

Nicky felt air move against him, and looked around. Joel was standing there with big, big eyes.

He was reading it. His face got all different colors, and he started to put his hand on the keys, but Nicky grabbed the receiver and hung up. The TDD light went out.

"Terrible, terrible," Joel signed, "You bad, bad, bad," and pulled Nicky out of the chair and hit his bottom. "Ask me! Why not?"

"Bored, me," Nicky signed, with his finger beside his nose. "Angry!" clawing his chest. "Not sorry!"

Then Marti ran in, and Joel pointed to the words. She put both hands on face, and rocked, rocked, like a rocking horse, til Joel shook her to make her stop.

Joel tried to explain TDDing to Marti, and she flapped mouth at the same time; Joel never let Nicky loose til Marti cried, and then Joel wrapped her up in his arms, and Nicky ran away.

Grandma caught him running out the door and said, "Chocolate cake for you," so he didn't run away right then. He ate cake, and then the news came on TV, and Joel said must watch it.

Joel sat right by the TV to interpret, but he kept looking over at Marti like afraid she was sick. She said they had to go tomorrow morning, very, very early. "Promise?" "Yes."

Then Grandpa made them all get in his car and drive by trees and trees. He stopped and pointed at Washington, DC, out there. They made Nicky tell the Presidents, but he got stuck after Washington, Jefferson, Lincoln, Kennedy, Roosevelt, Carter, Reagan. They looked at sunset and looked down steep cliffs that made you dizzy, but Joel and Marti didn't smile. Not much and not long, and Grandpa asked Nicky (hiding signs) why, and Nicky said Joel hugged Marti.

He didn't want to say "TDD" or tell what he did with it.

They drove to a church when he got hungry, and Nicky saw dinner on tables in lots of big dishes. Deaf people hugged Joel and shook Marti's hands and said, "Sit down and eat," so they did. No preaching came. So many people here, he found kids to talk to, and found out who were hearies. He watched

Marti. Her mouth was open a lot, and wide-eyes. She practiced signs that people taught her. Really funny, she tried so hard and made mistakes. One mistake made a dirty sign instead, and everybody laughed until one man said, "Not in church!" But it wasn't church, only church basement.

They drove home in dark, and Joel's hand lay on Nicky's neck til it felt like axe, cutting. Nicky had to get undressed when Joel did, and go to bed next to Joel on the porch in beds that folded. Joel said, "You run, you sorry!"

Nicky was dreaming Joel tied him to bed with rope around his neck, and he cried, but Joel leaned over and patted his head until he went to sleep again.

He'd never, never go back to Daddy, who was in Pittsburgh.

Marti

They didn't get away from Front Royal til ten a.m.

Joel found some backyard fence posts rotted at ground level and leaning. (It didn't help to have Hildie careening into them when she rough-housed with Nicky.) Five posts had to be replaced, before rabbits got into the garden. Then Joel cleaned out the roof gutters, while Marti anxiously held his ladder. Fretting. But how do you tell a sweet old couple their son mustn't take the time to do needed repairs for them?

Nicky grumbled and squirmed, squeezed between them in the cab of the truck while Marti drove. Much as she treasured Joel's tender comforting yesterday after they found Nicky type-telephoning to poor Alan Teague, she wouldn't give over the wheel to him today. They must end this journey in Pittsburgh, no place else.

"Come to think of it," she asked Joel suddenly, "if Alan has no deaf friends, why would he own a visual telephone-thing like your folks'?"

"Good question. The fire department and the police now have them, so he could get help in an emergency. And his mother has one. Of course."

Marti remembered what happened when they caught Nicky phoning.

Amazing. She'd expected such a brusque, bitter man to kiss her fiercely, demandingly, but he did not. He'd talked her back to her senses, and then held and rocked her for five minutes before he gave her one gentle, cautious, astonishingly gentle kiss.

It had almost put Alan's pain out of her thoughts.

"Marti hates you," Nicky told the man, and she'd read the shocked and hurt reply, right there in black on yellow. In Alan's possession, Joel explained, was an identical typescript: "Marti hates you."

And the other shocker: Lanier Strathgordon was now in Pittsburgh.

They'd have to keep Nicky very close. A pity the boy knew about that scary fact, but because he'd called Alan, they could at least be prepared to confront the father . . . who could lay claim to Nicky.

Nicky twisted around, kneeling to face backwards into the camper. Next he turned and sat with his heels drawn up on the seat, pounding his fists on his knees, glowering at the highway ahead. She should have Hildie up here, to amuse him. Then he slid down into the footspace and sat on Joel's feet for awhile. Marti was negotiating the tollway entrance and didn't see him til the moment Nicky reared up between Joel's legs, holding in his hands the cut cord from the bedroom drapes.

She pulled over quickly, as if she'd heard an approaching ambulance, eased the truck to a roll, and let other cars past. Nicky stood there, his face white. He looked first at Joel, then at her, and his small hands flew open. The long cord dropped on his feet, and he leaped into Joel's arms as if it were a rattlesnake.

"Oh, Nicky!" Marti cried, stretching a hand toward him, but Joel was already embracing the child who hung on his neck.

"Does he remember? Oh, Lord, Joel, what sort of memories—your dad said Nicky thought his head was chopped off."

"I don't know. I don't know," said Joel.

"I should have thrown the cord away!"

"No. No, if there's anything to keep his father off it'll be that cord, with the knot still in it, and the rope-burn—what's left of it—on his neck."

"But for me to have tossed it there- Oh, I'm sorry."

"I don't like his reaction," Joel admitted. "Wish we had a tranquilizer for him."

Marti started the truck moving again, down the Pennsylvania Turnpike, west.

"Are you ever going to talk to Nicky about it?" she asked. "The suicide-attempt?"

Without replying, Joel turned Nicky around so the boy sat facing him, straddling his knees. He shot Marti a drowning-man's look before he signed, then said, "What happened, Nicky? What scared you?"

Nicky's fingers flew to his neck. A doleful expression.

"Your neck got hurt the last time you saw your father?"

Nicky shook his head I-don't-know.

"He isn't married to your mother, now. But he still loves you. He was wrong; he was bad to you, but he didn't know any better."

Marti couldn't believe her ears.

"Want to talk about what's scaring you?"

Joel murmured, "I want to live with you forever."

This startled Marti, til she saw that Joel was no longer signing, Nicky was. Nicky had said that.

"You marry Marti. I want to be your son."

Joel didn't look at her. Color rose in his neck, but he didn't tell the child to be quiet.

"You don't have any little boy. Please keep me. Please keep me for yours."

"We can't, Nicky," Joel responded. "You have your own mother. I'm sure she loves you very much."

Nicky's lower lip protruded. He put his hands over his face. Marti looked for the curtain cord, but Joel had kicked it backwards under the seat. She didn't want to think what Joel might say when they next stashed Nicky in the camper.

When Nicky was persuaded to ride up over their heads, again, with Hildie for company and with the door to the camper locked, she found Joel uncommunicative.

"We need gas," he finally said. "There should be a station coming up along here pretty soon. I'll get us something to drink. Want a candy bar as well?"

She said yes; then, not looking away from the narrow turnpike lanes, "Don't you ever date deaf girls?"

"Huh? Sure I have."

"I imagine your folks would prefer that you—" She stopped.

"Lots of problems," he said. "Some deaf people don't want a live-in interpreter. Some deaf people also, down deep, prefer deaf children like them. Aside from the fact almost all deaf marry deaf, I doubt it would work out."

She said nothing.

"Besides, I've already got lousy genes."

"What?" She thought of hemophilia or muscular dystrophy.

"Mom's family's full of deaf people, going way back."

"She told me. But you better not call Nicky 'lousy,' Joel. Not to me."

"Nicky's already born. He's fantastic. One of a kind. But produce another kid to face a hearing society? I dunno. Social Responsibility, you can call it, or empathy in advance for any deaf kid."

"But you'd make a super father for one. Look at you."

He ignored that. "Frank's wife was rubella-deafened, so she won't pass anything on. Frank's genes alone did it for little Joel, and then he went and had another kid—"

"Little Joel?" she interrupted. "Named after you?"

"They might have had still another deaf kid, but baby Miriam is hearing."

"You say you want all deaf kids taken away from hearing parents, Joel. Well, I get the feeling you also want that hearing niece for yourself."

"I never said that."

"I'll bet you're thinking it, though. Another two-year-old interpreter for three deaf people, right? Miriam is you all over again, right?"

"Marti, you don't pull punches, do you?"

She backed off, let him up. "Nicky may have deaf kids, then?"

"Highly unlikely. He's the first one in his family-tree, he said." He didn't pursue the topic of baby Miriam and little Joel in California. He announced, "I'm waiting for a woman already with kids of her own, or one who doesn't want any."

Marti kept her gaze straight ahead.

"But I don't go telling any deaf woman that."

Marti spotted a filling station and headed off the turnpike. Joel made for the row of coin-op dispensers, while she unlocked the camper door and got her headscarf, to tame her tangle of wind-mangled hair.

For a moment she'd forgotten Nicky—their conversation had been too gripping, but Joel hadn't. He came back with three candy bars and three bottles of pop.

He gave her a choice, she took mints and an orange soda, and Joel stuck his head under the hood beside the attendant.

Waiting for him to emerge, she saw Hildie running to her, the worry-lines in her dog-face almost like a frown. Hildie darted to the roadside and back again to Marti.

The camper door stood open, no Nicky inside.

"Nicky's GONE!" she shouted at Joel.

"Find him! Find him!" she shrieked.

Joel dashed around the camper. He didn't yell "Nicky!" the way she did on her circuit of the station, checking restrooms and lube room.

She came to a halt on the edge of the buzzing stream of traffic, swiveling her whole body from right to left.

A little head was bobbing along beyond the waist-high center divider. He'd crossed through lanes of fast traffic?

"Nicky! There he is, Joel!"

Joel whipped around at her cry, and began loping toward Nicky, looping between speeding cars, holding back for a van to pass, then doing broken-field running across the next lanes. A good runner, thank God.

Marti's palms were nail-cut as she watched Joel come carrying Nicky slowly back across the highway, waiting patiently now for each lane to clear.

The boy was sweaty, cold to her touch, and beyond either scolding or comfort. Was this another break for freedom, or a second suicide-attempt? Joel asked that with sunken eyes and a wretched expression. Nicky had even run away from him.

"Any kid of mine take chances like that, I'd whale his bottom good," commented the station attendant, as Marti drove around behind the station to park.

They laid Nicky on the camper bed and sat facing him.

Joel found words before Marti could.

"Nicky," he signed, then muttered, "You don't have to see Daddy. No Daddy. Do you have a minister? From church? A special, favorite teacher?"

Nicky offered no suggestions.

Marti touched Joel's shoulder for encouragement. He signed again, without speech, his face complementing his hands. Nicky gazed at him, eyes bleak. Finally he spelled something on the fingers of his small right hand.

Joel asked another silent question, and got in return a wrist-tapping sign.

"What's that mean?" asked Marti.

"His doctor. Doctor Howell," Joel said.

"Do you think he'd help us?"

"We can call him. That's the most we can do."

Nicky signed again, touched his ear, then put flat hands side by side.

"His doctor," Joel translated, "is deaf."

Marti was startled into exclaiming, "Nicky's cat and his doctor BOTH are deaf?"

"Apparently so."

Nicky hadn't wanted his candy. Hildie got the peanut-log—an earned reward. (Two gulps.)

This time Marti held Nicky while Joel drove. The boy lay against her as still and lifeless as the time they'd driven with Mr. Strathgordon home to his house. That first Nicky-night. If only he didn't know Daddy had gone to Pittsburgh; Daddy might not even still be there. What could Daddy do? Take a swing at Joel? Strike a woman—the kidnapper once his friendly babysitter? Worst of all, what would he say? No, he couldn't say anything to Nicky. What would he DO to Nicky?

"A doctor," Joel said. "What chance he'd have more than ten minutes for Nicky? I wished he'd picked a priest or minister."

"Are you religious?"

"Not especially, but churches seem always to manage to understand, whether it's 'I believe' in voice or in Sign. I didn't know there was another deaf M.D. around, and I hear everything. A terrific doctor at Gallaudet College—for the deaf—died of the tumors that deafened him."

Close enough to Pittsburgh to find a city directory, Joel took Nicky into a phone booth, to help him locate the right doctor. It wasn't an unusual name.

They came back crestfallen. "No Howell. No M.D. named that, or optometrist, chiropractor, or podiatrist."

"How about dentist?"

"There's a different sign for dentist. Nicky said doctor."

"Well, what'll we do?"

Nicky climbed into the truck with his face set in the darkest scowl she'd seen for a week. He remained motionless for only a mile or two, then he began signing, so Joel had to pull over to understand.

"He's in a hospital. Nicky says he works at a hospital. That would explain why he's not in the book, then. A staff-doctor, maybe."

"But what hospital?"

Nicky understood her, instantly. He gestured for time to think, holding his head between small hands. "Hospital," he must be murmuring. "Hospital?"

Joel cracked his knuckles, one by one, waiting.

The letters came so slowly off Nicky's fingers, Marti herself might have read them from her Girl Scout experience with the alphabet.

"Okay. Great," Joel said. "That's enough. Half a name. We can get it from that."

Amazingly, he did. The next stop at a phone booth took him longer, and Nicky and Marti sat in the truck holding onto each other, watching. Twenty yards away, Joel's mouth moved. Talk, talk, talk. She wished he'd think to sign, too, so Nicky could write down for her what luck they were having.

When Joel came back, his eyes shone.

"Got him. He's an intern—can you believe that?—at a major hospital, here. 'Deaf as a post' some secretary admitted. A young guy. Dr. Keegan Howell. I asked how long he'd been deaf, but the woman didn't know."

"So he's not practicing yet? How would Nicky—"

Joel cocked a brow at her. "A deaf physician—how could he not be used all the time for deaf patients? Think of it!"

She knew she'd get another lecture, but every tale he told hit closer to home. (To heart, rather.) As a small boy, Joel had interpreted for his mother when the doctor found a lump in her breast; for his father, on the charming topic of hemorrhoids. Embarrassment all around. She could imagine. "Let's go. Straight to the hospital to find this Dr. Howell. How's he getting around the stethoscope problem?" Joel muttered.

It was past rush-hour, but the highways were narrower than Marti liked, bounded with walls and dividers. Thank heavens it was still daylight. They zoomed across a river, the Monongahela or something equally melodious, under clear skies surprising to her in the Steel City she'd never before visited. Up hills and down again they climbed to find the hospital.

Once there, they had no luck. "Try Dr. Howell's apartment, down the hill." Check! Joel backed the camper out of the lot again, and Marti read him his own scribbled directions. "There. Over there, that complex."

"Pray," he said. "I don't look forward to walking in on Nicky's clan tonight any more than he does."

"What are the chances, Joel, that we'll get arrested? For child-stealing?"

He visibly flinched. "I'm damned sorry you're along. Dragging you into it—I told everyone you weren't involved."

"Well, this is your only transportation. Abandon me somewhere, and you'll still arrive in my truck, with my license-plates. You also forget, Joel, that I was the one to run away with Nicky. You joined the caravan rather late. You can't take all the credit—"

"Saint Joel, huh?" He didn't smile.

All three of them rode the elevator up to the apartment with a mailbox saying, "Howell-Fallon."

"Hmmm. Regular guy, then? Living with a lady he's not married to?"

"Or he has a liberated wife."

When he touched the doorbell, Marti asked, "How will he hear it ring?"

"He'll manage."

When the doctor's door opened, an attractive blonde young woman smiled them across the threshold, motioning them in. She immediately flicked signs to Nicky.

"You already know each other?" Marti cried. "How wonderful! And you can sign, too!"

"Sure, if she lives here," said Joel, furnishing the girl their names. "And you are—?"

She didn't speak. She spelled with dazzling speed.

"Cindy Fallon," Joel said. "She's deaf, too. Keegan Howell is married to her sister Leslie."

"I see," said Marti, astonished.

The girl was small, slender, and smiling, wearing jeans and a red western shirt. She led them through a modern living-room to a snug kitchen nook. Nicky came right along, hanging to her shirt-tail.

Joel spoke for Cindy: "I babysit Nicky. Keegan just called. He'll be back about seven. A lady's been in an auto-wreck, and he had to tell her that her husband's dead."

"Oh, awful!" Marti moaned.

Cindy must be hardened to such news. She darted to the electric range and bent to draw a pie pan out of the oven, her hand swaddled in dishtowel. She set it on the table and fanned it, grinning, a lovely, fair-skinned teenager with sunshine-hair. Marti felt her curiosity rise. One expected only old people to be deaf, but Olga Dalton must have once been like this. The girl slit a bag of marshmallows and dropped them over the sweet-potato pie as she talked to Joel, first on one hand, then the other, without moving her lips. Her eyes talked, and her elfin face and mobile brows.

"Keegan's busy all the time," Joel murmured, restraining Nicky from the pie til it was whisked back into the oven. "Busy, busy. And tired. His wife—my sister—is working. She won't be home until late. I am studying welding." (Cindy squinted and aimed a torch at them.)

"Welding?" Was that the sign? Ah, emancipation!

Cindy put out a teapot and four mugs, explaining that when people came to find Keegan she fed them. Nicky, unfed since lunch, watched her pour lemonade into his mug.

"I love welding. The sparks are so pretty, and the men all flirt with me," she said, fluttering eyelash-fingers at Joel.

Marti felt a tremor of anxiety. Jealousy? Conversation bubbled around her, Nicky contenting himself with lemonade and never taking his eyes off Cindy and Joel.

They all got sweet potato pie, and Cindy poured tea. Unlike Nicky, she made no sounds and hardly ever moved her lips. But her hands danced as if directed by a very good choreographer.

When Marti smiled and rubbed her stomach, Joel taught her "Thank you," kissing the hand outward from the chin. Why hadn't she asked for that sign at the Daltons', instead of merely mouthing thanks?

Nicky looked capable of summoning a smile by the time Dr. Howell arrived. Joel sprang up at the buzzer and the apartment's madly flashing lights. He beat Cindy to the door.

Nicky ran to the young doctor in a white jacket over a blue shirt, just as Marti heard him say, "Sorry I've made you wait to see me."

In a perfectly normal voice.

Dr. Howell might have been Cindy's own brother, not her brother-in-law, he was so blonde and blue-eyed. A little taller than Joel, with a turned-up nose that took years off his probable age.

"You're recently deafened, then?" Joel asked, hands moving. "I figured that."

Marti rushed in with her own questions: "Do you know Nicky's mother? Do you like her? It's a terrible situation we're in—"

And then she realized he didn't understand what she'd said.

"I'm no speechreader," Dr. Howell said cheerfully. "You'll have to utilize your interpreter."

Before Joel could move, Marti asked him, "When did you go deaf?" (Hands covering her ears.)

"I got too near a land-mine. It exploded. Overseas."

"In Viet Nam?"

"What was that?"

Joel's hands caught up with her.

"Oh. You asked WHEN. Six years ago. Yes, in 'Nam. One's voice can be maintained for a decade or so," he said wryly. "I fool people, as long as they allow me a monologue."

He set Nicky on the edge of the table among the tea mugs to examine the boy's neck, raising his eyes to watch, behind Nicky, Joel's rapid signing to accompany his story.

"Nicky tried to hang himself a week ago. With a curtain cord. His father had him, and forbade Sign or even writing, the bastard. Nicky's had no medical checkup. Mainly he won't talk sense about the hanging, so we're worried."

"Understandable," the doctor said.

"Just now he made another run for it, across the Turnpike. A close call. Two weeks ago he ran away from his dad and walked for twenty hours." He started to explain about Nicky's mother, but was interrupted.

"I know. I know the family, all but the father."

Marti wondered if Keegan had children, and what kind. Not deaf ones. He'd had his ear-drums blown in. Poor, poor man.

"Let me have a little chat alone with Nicky," the doctor said. "Come on, pal."

He led the boy away, carrying a cup of coffee Cindy had rushed into his free hand. They went into another room, and the door closed behind them.

"What'd you think of HIM?" Joel asked. "Sorry he's already taken?"

"What?" Marti found herself blushing.

"I saved him," Cindy said.

"You certainly did," Marti through Joel replied. "Did you see Nicky gorge himself on your good pie?"

"No, I saved KEEGAN's life," she corrected them. "I taught Keegan signs when he was so mad you couldn't get near him. I wasn't afraid. Then Leslie married him, and I live with them during welding school."

That must be a tale and a half, Marti figured.

When Joel pumped her about Keegan's difficulties in medical school, she said sister Leslie knew as much medicine now as he did. She'd interpreted for him all the way.

No, no children. "No time for them!" Cindy laughed.

Until doctor and patient reappeared, Joel amused Cindy with a description of the marathon, putting into graphic signs the mob of runners, the press to the starting line, the pistol, the long, exhausting race, the cups of ERG, the awards. Cindy sparkled, shooting him questions, grinning charmingly. Flirting. He asked how old she was. Nineteen.

A rubella baby, she said. Her mother had had German measles. Leslie was her support-system, not her parents. "And sister Leslie's reward," Marti mused, "was Dr. Keegan Howell? Not bad!"

Keegan Howell came back.

"Okay. I get the picture, I think." When the child's attention was distracted by Cindy's visual gossip, he confided, "Nicky hasn't much recall. Blocked, or whatever my colleagues in psychiatry would call it. A pity there isn't time to have him see more of an authority than I."

"We don't know who's at home, now," Joel said.

"I'll go over there. After you telephone and see what's up." The doctor furnished them the Strathgordon number, and after Joel dialed, Marti took the receiver away from him. "My job," she said, sounding twice as brave as she felt.

A kid answered, who sounded like a teenage girl.

Yes, her father was there, she said blithely. Waiting for Mom to get back. Kirby just left to pick up Mom and Steve at the airport.

Marti didn't tell her anything. She sure didn't sound like a girl with any worries. Or with a kidnapped kid brother.

"What's she like?" Joel asked, as they sat around the coffee table, drinking Cindy's various brews.

"The mom? Jane helps at Nicky's school, she's in all the deaf associations, she preaches Total Communication to parents. She's learning ASL, too, but no adult is going to be as fluent in that language as Nicky and Cindy."

"You don't think of ASL as 'broken Enlgish,' do you?" Joel asked him, frowning.

"Of course not. Its only disadvantage is that it can't be written down—except in symbols." He paused, looking quizzically at Joel, as if he wanted to say much more.

"Cindy has sat for Nicky. I've known the family eight or nine months. Everyone gets sick sometimes, and I meet sick deaf people pretty promptly."

"How about the suicide-attempt?" Joel asked. "What'll she do if she hears the truth?"

"Wouldn't her ex-husband tell her?"

"We don't know what the damned father has told her—if he could reach her—or told anybody else. I took Nicky away from him. He didn't see Nicky after the suicide-attempt, or see the hanging, either."

"And you, with deaf parents, mistreated as children, perhaps—" The young doctor softly said.

"My father was. Mom lucked out. A deaf family."

"Nicky's mom has to be told. Just the way Nicky has to remember it, himself; get it up out of his memory's dark cellar. It'll rot there, and color his life, maybe. Black. Pardon the Pop-Psychologizing. Nicky swore to me that he never saw a curtain-cord, never did himself harm. All he remembers is a big, bloody axe. From some movie thriller, I imagine."

They sat and stared at each other.

"I'm sure glad you came to me," Keegan Howell said. "Nine is a terrible age for a little boy to lose his mother to a new husband. I'm not up on the Oedipal stuff, but she's been with him constantly. Interpreting at his school, too. Signing everything you say is hard work. There's a limit to what any one person can do for another person who's handicapped; there were days I didn't think my marriage would survive—my wife is hearing. But she's a champ, and my ego has gotten tougher."

Marti looked down, embarrassed by his bluntness.

"She got me through med school—she and my rich uncle. Now—back to Nicky. Jane Strathgordon—what is it now, Bratt?—was a teacher before Nicky arrived, but she quit to stay home with him. Don't go barking up the wrong tree." He smiled. "Do people still use that expression?"

At that hint of humor, Marti stopped biting her tongue and asked, "How is it, for you? What do you miss most?"

Joel gave her a disapproving frown as he interpreted, but the young doctor gestured to him a calming motion. "Music," he said. "I miss music. I was learning to play the guitar. Then the telephone. Until more TDD's become available, that's a real disadvantage. But you learn to live with it." He glanced at Joel. "You can't stay enraged all your life; you'll burst a blood-vessel. You'll stroke-out."

"I'll need to call Leslie before I go." But when Marti made another grab for the telephone, he shook his head. "No. Sorry. There's no TDD where she's working, now."

It was Joel who took the receiver after Keegan dialed, and Joel who listened, and flickered his fingers at her husband, after Keegan explained the current emergency.

"I imagine you started interpreting very young," he observed, standing up and looking down at Joel. "Stick around. I'll go talk to Nicky's father, then you follow in an hour or so. I'll draw a map to help you find the place."

While he sketched city highways and by-ways, he continued talking. "I forgot to thank you for interpreting. It's easier than written messages. But it's never fun to use a go-between. Between a man and his wife."

Again that thoughtful pause. Marti watched the two men closely, Joel's childhood tales in her mind: Interpreting, interpreting, for the grocer, the banker, the police, the doctor. Trying to put hearies' curses into signs, weeping at insults his parents could not hear, calculating, covering up, fibbing to hearies sometimes, advising what car Dad should buy, calling carpenters, electricians, plumbers before the days of TDD's.

"So long," Dr. Howell said. "Before you come, Joel, try for a little empathy. Hard as that may be. Put yourself in Strathgordon's place. Just for an instant. He really loved his wife. When you meet her, you'll see why. Now he's lost her. Over Nicky. Forever."

Joel said very little during that one hour wait. He spoke Cindy's description of Florida, of boats and swimming, of boyfriends and animals. Nicky watched four winged hands flitting past.

"Very nice guy," Joel said, when he took the wheel of her truck, at her request. Night was falling. Nicky sat between them.

"Very good-looking, too, wouldn't you say?" His half-smile was wistful.

"Wise, as well."

"Cindy's a cutie. And deaf. Pure ASL. You gonna pair me off with her?"

"No!" she said too emphatically, and immediately added, "No; as you have noticed, I need someone to drive my truck in the dark. When I can't see a darned thing."

They fell silent, too much aware of what awaited them at Nicky's house. This was no jolly social call.

"Cindy rescued him. The doctor." Joel shook his head. "Think of that. She was sure proud to tell us."

"And now she's a welder, and he's a physician, M.D."

"Money Doctor," Joel said.

"He sure sounds like a man who'll earn it."

Nicky

Sitting between Joel and Marti, Nicky scowled at the road ahead. After nice deaf Grandma and Grandpa and the train and hugs and food, now Dr. Howell was gone to Daddy, and Joel and Marti were taking him away from Cindy into the black.

He didn't like the way Joel had looked worried, and Marti, too, and Doctor. He wanted to go away. Away, away, like a bird. His neck hurt. It would be all black at home, and hurt-neck and horrible.

Going home was happiness, Doctor told him, but why didn't Doctor smile?

Daddy would be there. Alan Teague said that. Joel didn't sign yes or no when he asked to be sure, but you can't fool a kid on something so important. Daddy was there. Mama would know he hated her, and be so mad she'd give him to Daddy to keep. You belong to Daddy or Mama, and they can give you to anyone they want. He'd have a new Step-daddy like old Daddy, and hands would be tied, and head chopped off, and hands chopped off, like astronaut's, and he'd rather die. Open the truck door and jump out and get squashed like Jack's kitten in the road. To look like scrambled eggs and tomatoes.

"She doesn't want me. She didn't die, and she didn't come help me, which shows she doesn't want me anymore."

He had to run away again. Go where no one would catch him.

He got more and more sick when he saw houses he knew, and then the truck slowed down. A car sat in front of his house, and Nicky looked at it hard. He thought he knew it. Closer up, it was blue.

Daddy's car.

"NO!" he said very loud, and Marti jumped. Joel and Marti were getting out of the truck. Nicky hooked one arm through the steering wheel and locked his hands on wrists, Indian-grip.

Joel came around to the sidewalk door and reached for him, signing short and fast to get out of the truck, right now.

Nicky wouldn't.

Joel took hold of his legs.

"No, no, no, NO!" Nicky shouted. "Daddy's car," he said, motioning with his head because his fingers were locked on arms.

Joel pulled on his legs to come. He'd forgotten how Daddy's car looked, but Nicky would never forget that big, long, ugly blue car that chased them here from Knoxville. His neck hurt bad.

Then Joel tried to pull his hands loose, and Nicky bit him. Joel swatted his rear so fast, he was too surprised to cry. Then Joel pulled him loose, because he was stronger, and dragged Nicky across the seat.

"Stay with you! Stay with you!" Nicky cried. "No Mama! No Daddy! I hate here. Here will kill me!"

He thought they'd spank him, but Joel began to stroke him, and Marti came and kissed. Nicky hugged her tight around the neck and locked hands on wrists again. She went tremble, tremble. Joel patted him, and they stood still a minute, but Doctor came out of the house, and they started moving, Joel holding Nicky, and Nicky leaning over and hanging onto Marti's neck like for death.

Nicky's eyes were shut when they went through door. Outdoor-smells became house-smells that he knew. But he wouldn't look. Hands came on him, and he cried, "No, no, no," and tears ran down.

They were in the livingroom, and he saw his sisters. Kirby wore a football shirt number 24 with his face all twisted up. Hands turned Nicky around, and he saw Mama with red face, and tears.

She said his name with her mouth, over and over, and signed his name on her heart, but he turned away his face, and grabbed Joel's arm. Hands and more hands touched him and squeezed him, and it was warm with bodies. He wanted to throw up.

Then Dr. Howell picked him up. He knew, because doctors' hands always smell like soap.

He wiped his eyes. Joel and Marti were standing close together. Against other wall, frowning, with arms crossed, stood Daddy.

Nicky held his neck and screamed. Screamed and screamed, and Dr. Howell turned his face tight against his shirt, so it was like eating shirt. His stomach went bang down to the floor. He hit his doctor. He hit, hit, hit the people who held him, and yelled "No, no, no!"

It wasn't fair. He was too little to go where he wanted or to stay where he wanted with who he wanted. It wasn't FAIR!

He fought to get to Joel and Marti, who looked like leaving, now, but Doctor wouldn't let him.

Steve Bratt came over and squatted down and spelled on his hand, "Welcome home, son," with the E like O and the N like M, that he could figure out from "Wolcomo homo, som."

Steve's mustache was cut away from his lips.

Nicky didn't care. Didn't care! He felt smothered, and his neck hurt, hurt, hurt, choking. Daddy didn't move. Not even his eyes.

Doctor kept Nicky's head in his big, soapy hand, and didn't make him go to Daddy. Doctor talked, talked, talked over Nicky's head, his chest like an engine going.

When he looked around finally, Joel was still there, and Marti, and Mama. Daddy, too. Bad Daddy, not Steve. They were sitting down. Doctor put Nicky on the couch and sat down by him. He grabbed a pillow to hug in front of him, to watch all of them over the top of it.

Doctor said, "Nicky, you will live with Mama, not with Daddy. Daddy won't take you back to Knoxville. He can't." (Dropping his finger down to hit his other finger, hard. "CAN'T.")

Then he said, "You don't need to go see him unless you want to. When you grow up."

Daddy didn't move, and Nicky peeked at him. His face was dark and sad-ugly. His shoulders hung down. He was watching Doctor's hands like they were doing magic.

"You are a lucky boy, Nicky," said Doctor. "You have many people who love you. Some make mistakes, but they still love you."

Nicky didn't believe it.

"Big people aren't always right," Doctor signed. "Daddy is sorry. He is going away, now, but he wanted to see you home safe."

Mama wanted to talk to him, Nicky saw, but she didn't dare. She looked at Doctor and looked at him and Daddy, and sat on the edge of her chair with her knees together and her hands knotty, and her face shiny-wet.

"Tell me something," Dr. Howell said in very slow, small signs after he put Nicky standing in front of him with his back to the other people so they couldn't see what Doctor signed. "Did someone hurt your neck?"

It was what he had asked in apartment, and Nicky was scared. He didn't know. He didn't know.

Doctor's face looked sad. "Sometimes people hurt themselves, when no one saves them. Children do."

Doctor put his hands very gentle on Nicky's cheeks, like ladies do, to kiss you, and then his hands slid down Nicky's neck. His neck hurt, and he choked. He closed his eyes and felt tight on neck, and black, and fall, fall, fall, and he started to cry.

"Did you hurt yourself? To go away? To die?" Doctor asked on his hands.

"Yes!" Nicky sobbed.

"You don't need to do that ever again," he said. "You are safe, now. Safe, safe, safe," Doctor signed.

Then Doctor looked up and made mouth, and Marti came and gave him keys. Doctor picked up Nicky and carried him away. Outside to the camper. He unlocked the back door, and Hildie kissed both of them, wagging and standing up.

Doctor got in camper and took something in his hand that Nicky couldn't see. Doctor's face said worry, worry, in street-light. He leaned down near Nicky and signed, "Look," and opened up his hand.

"What is this, Nicky?"

"Hurt me!" Nicky said.

"Throw it away," Doctor mimed, and pretended to throw the long white rope in Marti's trash-box. Nicky watched; he couldn't breathe.

"You throw away?" to Nicky, eyebrows up, handing the thing toward him.

Nicky didn't want it. To touch it. He knew what it was. He saw the knot he tied. A snake with a knot in it. His neck hurt. His heart went Bam, Bam, Bam, and Doctor's arms went tighter around him. Snakes kill you. Bite your neck. He hit at it, but Doctor pulled it away so he couldn't reach it. Then he laid it in Nicky's lap.

"Take it," he signed, "and YOU throw it away. Then it can't hurt you anymore. CAN'T."

He waited. So did Nicky.

Nicky reached down fast, grabbed the rope, and threw it hard right into the trash.

"All gone!" Doctor signed, like "finish." "All gone, and can't ever hurt you again."

Doctor took Nicky out of the camper and back into the house, then.

Daddy's mouth went teethy-teethy, and Nicky looked at Daddy and didn't understand. He looked at Mama, and Mama signed for Daddy, "I'm sorry. I wanted to be good to you. I love you, son."

Nicky didn't move.

"My wife Annalee and I both love you, Nicky. We only tried to help you."

Mama's eyes went very wet, and then Nicky's did, too. He didn't want Daddy to touch him, though.

Daddy stood up. Mama started to get up, and then she came to Nicky, almost like crawling, and knelt down in front of him. Him and Doctor.

"Left me," Nicky's fingers spelled, like talking to self, but Mama saw it.

"I lived alone to help you a long, long, long time," she signed. "Because I love you. I gave you all, all, all of me. You need a father. I need a husband. Steve loves you. He signs already. You teach him."

"Daddy s don't learn," Nicky said in ASL, but she understood.

Mama turned to Daddy, and signed very slow, "Teach me, Nicky." then Nicky saw Daddy sign, very hearie: "Teach me, Nicky."

Nicky shut his eyes for a minute, to breathe.

"You're a big boy," Mama signed, trying to do ASL: "Grow-finish. Boy-big." Then she said, "You must not be a baby, any-more. Mama must live, too. You teach Steve signs, and I will teach Steve signs, and someday maybe even Daddy will learn. Think about your brother and sisters. They love you. They missed you."

"Trust?" Nicky signed, fist on fist.

"Trust me, yes. Trust all of us. And forgive your Daddy."

Mama leaned closer. Her face got nearer and nearer, all wet, and Nicky decided she needed him. He touched her wet face and then kissed it. Doctor squeezed him like good, good. Mama picked him up. He was too big for her, so he got down, but he hugged onto Mama to hold her up. She didn't stand up very well; she wasn't even big as Marti.

He turned around and saw Joel walking, and Marti got up, and they went toward the door. Nicky hurried and hugged them, and kissed Marti, and then they pushed him, push, push, back toward Mama.

Daddy had white face with lines. He wanted to shake hands.

"Don't tie hands. Don't ever hurt me again," Nicky signed, and looked at Mama, but she didn't make flutter-lips for Daddy.

Doctor didn't either. Daddy showed teeth and looked like crying; Nicky didn't want him to cry. Everybody was looking.

Nicky didn't say anything more. He shook Daddy's hand like big men do, and then he went to Mama. Daddy went away.

Joel waved a little wave goodbye, and then they went away, too. Nicky forced himself to stand still and not cry.

Elyse came back holding the sort of ice-cream bar he liked best, and after he took it, he saw Doctor go away, after signing "Proud, proud of you. Big boy, now."

He'd see Doctor again, very soon, and write to Joel and Marti, and Leah and Kirby were here, now, too, but he knew he wouldn't see Daddy again. Not unless he wanted to. To teach Daddy to talk to him.

Steve hugged Nicky suddenly from behind, and picked him up to the ceiling, so Nicky almost dropped his ice cream. He knew who, because Steve's hands had freckles.

"I like your new friends," Mama signed to him. "Good people."

"I wanted to be their son, before," he said, careful to use "wanted," and "before," not "want" or "now."

"They're young people. They'll have their own little boy, one day," said Mama.

"Hope," said Nicky.

"Thank you for shaking Daddy's hand," Mama said, stopping crying. "He will always remember that."

"It didn't hurt me," said Nicky.

And then he saw his ice cream bar was melting, so he had to hurry and eat it.

Marti & Joel

"For a moment like this one, I can think of only three good remedies," Joel said, a mile from the house where they'd left Nicky.

Marti made not one sound, sitting rigid with fists locked together between her knees. He was glad he was driving; otherwise, he might crumple up. He had to stop, now, to help Marti. And himself.

He took hold of her hand, pried it free of her other hand.

"One choice: We can go out and get roaring drunk. Or lock up the truck and take a nice long run. Or we can bed down somewhere."

She sighed. "I . . . I'm having a hard enough time just . . . not crying." He wouldn't guess how much her tears were for him.

"Choose," he said in a falsely bright voice.

"A run," she whispered. "That's my profession."

"Done. Give me a minute to get into shorts."

It was dark. They'd been in that house a long time; it was after eleven. She didn't want to remember the faces. Such wretched guilt and remorse and horror she never wanted to see again. And the blessed doctor, talking so softly and steadily, soothing Jane Bratt and Lanier Strathgordon, analyzing their son's suicide-attempt, talking on his hands to Nicky when he was not caressing the child. Performing the catharsis, the cauterization, taking Nicky out to see and understand the suicide-weapon, saying, "Psychiatrists might condemn me for this, but I think he needs it made as real and visible to him as manual language."

Talk about acting-out! Talk about drama!

And to face Lanier Strathgordon, watch him twitch and suffer, and hear him groan to see Nicky's hatred—how glad she was that she'd gone to him at the end, after all of them left, she and Joel promising to visit Nicky next month.

He was not waiting to waylay them, sitting there limp in his car. He hadn't told anyone Nicky's troubles, or even that Nicky was MISSING. She went around to his side, and put her hands on the windowframe.

"Mr. Strathgordon," she'd begun, and . . . ended.

He sat staring at her, waiting. She knew by his eyes how far down he was, and felt no more anger with him. She sensed Joel standing in the empty street behind her.

"Your son will understand you better as he gets older. I think he forgives you, already," she said.

"Do you think so?" he whispered, looking up at her.

"I'm sure of it. You only meant to help him. We all learned a lot tonight. All of us. Every one."

"Alan admitted the truth. About his childhood; having heard, all that. He came to Annalee after you telephoned him; she told me today over the phone."

"I telephoned him? That was Nicky on the TDD."

She explained what happened. "I don't hate Alan. Poor man, he needs friends. You could help HIM. He may need you even more than Nicky does."

"That deaf doctor," Lanier said, "he didn't even read lips, but he—" and he fell silent.

"Alan ought to meet him!" she said.

"But I can't . . . we can't . . . come to visit Nicky? Ever?"

"Not yet," she said. "Not for awhile, I'd think."

Joel moved her aside and slipped his hand into the car.

"I hope things go well for you," he said, through the tensest throat Marti'd ever heard. He had his hand on Mr. Strathgordon's shoulder.

"Thank you," Nicky's father said quietly.

As he drove away, Lanier Strathgordon did not look back.

Joel's clothes-changing made the truck sway a little, keeping Marti aware of him. His sorrow bruised her heart. She couldn't think about it any longer, or think about that other man who'd tonight had to relinquish Nicky.

Joel returned, opened her door, and practically lifted her down from the seat. "Get changed," he said. "I want to see you run, for once. A ten-minute miler must need improvement. Coaching." He pushed her toward the camper door.

She got slowly out of her jeans and into knit shorts, pulling white socks halfway up to her knees. Her limbs wouldn't half move. It felt like swimming through glue. She came around the truck to find him stretching against a lamp post, making a lean-to of his body. Hard body. Good legs. Very brown. Wearing an extra Pine Mountain Marathon shirt. She hadn't half looked at him, before.

"Ah," said Joel. "Very nice."

But this was no time to come on to her, he decided. Better shut up. Clam up. While she was in mourning at least. While HE was in mourning. But he appreciated the bubble-bottom and the cheerleader's legs.

"Let's jog," he said.

"All three of us," she said, and showed him how her big mutt Hildie could jog, too—heeling perfectly without a leash.

They ran through the starlight, looking down the mountain on the river below them, full of orange lights. What a gorgeous view he had chosen, the whole city beneath them.

"You know Pittsburgh?" she asked, pulling abreast.

"Sure. Mom's residential school's here. She comes back often."

"Not the same as Nicky's school—Lynnwood."

"No, that's a new one. Look—U.S. Steel."

The tall building, wrapped in golden lights and dotted at the top with red ones, made her think of jewels in black velvet. Mirrored, rippling, in the water.

"There are a hundred bridges over the three rivers in Pittsburgh," he said.

Marti and Hildie ran on the inside, tucked behind his left shoulder. Their shoes made hardly a smack-smack on the roadway. Like one horse; four human feet equal one horse. A few dogs barked, but not very enthusiastically. He led and she followed, noting how low he carried his arms, how straight his back, how economical and regular his stride. Anybody could recognize a marathoner. She wondered if he ran ultra-marathons. She wondered if they could ever come back and see Nicky.

When cars using cross-streets made them stop, he dropped his arm around her shoulders and squeezed. Neither spoke.

Some of the neighborhoods weren't exactly safe, she suspected, but they were going faster, not talking anymore. Joel had lengthened his stride, and she made herself keep pace, breathing harder, liking the ache. Let her legs ache for once, not her heart.

More cars. "You seem to know the route. You've run here, before?"

"I run everywhere," he said. "Just like you."

The night smelled sweet and fresh. They approached an eight-minute mile. Therapy—pure therapy.

He led her past houses, warehouses, up and down hills, into the light and back into the dark. If she hadn't fixed her gaze on his green back, she would not have been able to negotiate this long, unfamiliar course. Not with her night-vision. At the speed she could manage, Joel wasn't even starting to perspire. She wondered, though, about showers. His-and-Her showers. Where?

Anywhere.

She was totally lost, as she might have expected, when she found herself within half a block of her camper. He led her into a near-collision with her own vehicle.

"Let's not stop yet," she said. "I don't want to think."

So they kept on, and she moved up and ran shoulder to shoulder with him. Second wind. Body on automatic pilot.

He took her hand like racers who come across the line together, hand in hand, to tell you they intend a tie. Maybe they would someday make a pair. Eventually, Joel and she. After all, they'd together had a child, and lost one. Maybe they deserved to see each other once in awhile. Run together, at least. Maybe Joel was the one she'd waited for so long.

"I'd like to meet your brother," she said at another crossing, just to see what Joel said.

"He's a deafie," he said wryly, grinning. "I've got such impressive deaf kinfolk, you might find one you'd like better than me."

She ran closer to him, so her right arm brushed his, and he took her hand again. Such a little hand, he was thinking, but it might surprise him. It might be able to learn so much, so fast. Both her hands. His heart seemed to stretch itself inside him, like a cat, and purr.

He looked down, under a streetlight smiling that sad-eyed smile at her. His lips said (maybe they said, she couldn't see well enough to be sure), maybe he said, "I love you."

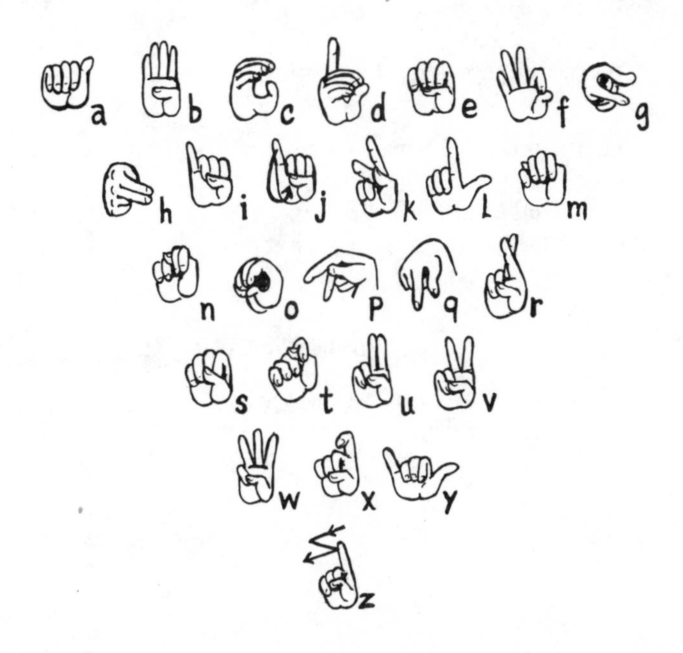

I need to perceive life through native eyes,
  not yours which are, after all, yours.
You're sailing on a vastly foreign sea
It's my country — you're the stranger,
Listen to me.

We sign a language all our own
Our hands are yours to share
The word, I think, is communication
And more than that, communion . . .
We speak through sign and both together
Whatever and by all the means
To the end.

Millions of stars do not make me a star
Millions of communists do not mean you
  must go that way
The pilgrims were a handful on a newfound shore
That was their own.

Let me choose if I will
To be different from the mass
Learn that there is beauty in a single star
Peace and grace in being what you are.

Mervin D. Garretson

from "The Deaf Child"

THE BALLET OF THE HANDS

By Lawrence Newman

OBSERVE:
How fingers curl and paint
Until out of airy nothingness
Words and pictures leap and dance
With wondrous grace and beauty of design
The ballet of the hands.

REFLECT:
An open door, a ray of light,
A history of struggle to survive
The choking confines of man's mind
Until thrive in home and meeting place
Hands that sculpture, talk, and sing,
Our very own. O palpable air!

THINK:
Motionless or fluid, curled or uncurled,
One finger, one flick of the wrist,
One sweep of the hands can evoke
Happiness or grief, stir minds
As if by some magic alchemy,
O for such a gift raise your eyes and praise.

STUDY:
The face complementary, alive,
Vibrant the body, coiled or uncoiled
In muted chorus to the dancing hands,
All converging in three dimensional grace,
O communication sure and joyous!

SEE:
The ballet of the hands,
How they portray
A falling leaf with a feathery touch,
The force and power of Thor's thunder,
The parade of history in one hour,
The soft beauty of confessed love,
The word of God . . . O let us all arise
And in chorus sing a tableau of praise.

Appendix

Information about deafness and sign language is obtainable from the following resources:

NATIONAL ASSOCIATION OF THE DEAF, (NAD) 814 Thayer Avenue, Silver Spring, Maryland 20910, (301) 587-1788.

Publishes the DEAF AMERICAN magazine and the BROADCASTER newspaper monthly. Publishes and distributes sign-language texts, cards, and films, and materials on all aspects of deafness and the lives of deaf people. Catalog available.

(JUNIOR NAD, c/o Gallaudet College, 7th and Florida, N.E., Washington, D.C. 20002)

INTERNATIONAL ASSOCIATION OF PARENTS OF THE DEAF, (IAPD) 814 Thayer Avenue, Silver Spring, Maryland, 20910, (301) 585-5400

Publishes a bimonthly newsletter, the ENDEAVOR, and advises parents and the public on issues relevant to parents of the deaf.

GALLAUDET COLLEGE, 7th and Florida, N.E., Washington, D.C. 20002. Liberal Arts College for the deaf, Graduate School, research programs.

Sign Language Programs; Public Information service with brochures on many topics; Kendall School and the Model Secondary School for the Deaf serve pre-school to pre-college-age students. Bookstore catalog available.

NATIONAL TECHNICAL INSTITUTE FOR THE DEAF, One Lomb Memorial Drive, Rochester, New York 14623.

Affiliated with the Rochester Institute of Technology, Deaf students integrated with hearing. Interpreters and other programs for the deaf.

CALIFORNIA STATE UNIVERSITY, NORTHRIDGE, 18111 Nordhoff Street, Northridge, California, 91330.

Integrated deaf and hearing students, deaf programs and interpreters, Leadership Training Program for workers with the deaf.

REGISTRY OF INTERPRETERS FOR THE DEAF, (RID) 814 Thayer Ave., Silver Spring, MD 20910 (301) 588-2406.

Certifies interpreters and publishes a directory listing them.

NATIONAL CENTER FOR LAW AND THE DEAF, Florida Avenue at 7th, N.E., Washington, D.C. 20002, (202) 651-5000.

Distributes materials and advises upon civil rights and civil and criminal prosecution involving deaf people.

NATIONAL FRATERNAL SOCIETY OF THE DEAF, 1300 W. Northwest Highway, Mt. Prospect, Illinois 60056. (312) 392-9282; 392-1409, TDD.

Furnishes life insurance for the deaf and other services.

TELECOMMUNICATIONS FOR THE DEAF, INC., (TDI) 814 Thayer Ave., Silver Spring, MD 20910.

Coordinates acquisition and distribution of surplus teletypewriters to deaf people, publishes a newsletter and a directory of numbers.

NATIONAL THEATER OF THE DEAF, (NTD) 305 Great Neck Road, Waterford, Connecticut, 06385.

Touring company offering traditional and original dramas on stage and on television; signs and voice narration both used.

AMERICAN HUMANE ASSOC. HEARING DOG PROGRAM, 5351 S. Roslyn St., Englewood, CO 80111 (303) 779-1400, 770-5599 (TDD).

AMERICAN ANNALS OF THE DEAF, 5034 Wisconsin Avenue, N.W., Washington, D.C. 20016.

Scholarly articles on deafness, with a Spring index-issue listing all agencies and services for the deaf, nationwide.

Other Novels About The Deaf: *In This Sign,* Joanne Greenberg, *The Sounds of Silence,* Judith Richards, *Silent Witness,* Susan Yankowitz, *The Mermaid's 3 Wisdoms,* Jane Yolen (youth).

Nonfiction: *They Grow in Silence,* Mindel and Vernon, *Sound and Sign,* Schlesinger and Meadow, *Deaf Like Me,* Spradley and Spradley, *Deafness and Child Development,* Meadow.

Other Alinda Press Publications

Island of Silence, by Carolyn Brimley Norris. Popular Library, 1976; Alinda Press, 1978. The story of Keegan Howell and the Fallon sisters. Romantic suspense involving the problems of the born-deaf and the late-deafened.

("I enjoyed the book very much as literature and anyone who reads it will, I think, be struck by its good sense, realism, and humanity," Joanne Greenberg.)

Hardbound, $5.95, Softbound, $2.50

Letters From Deaf Students, ed. C. Norris. Gallaudet College students talk frankly about their parents, their education, and their problems. $1.00

Ben's Quiet World,
By Frank Caccamise, illustrated by C. Norris. A small guide in comic-book form for hearing children to help them understand deaf people and signing. $.60

Animals in Signs, Home in Signs, Community in Signs, and Food in Signs,
Large softbound sign-language primers, featuring sign, sign-description, word, and picture of object. Also alphabet, numbers, colors, preface and bibliography. Each, $2.50

Cope Book
A collection of 45 useful basic signs for hospital personnel, baby-sitters, and others who serve the deaf, and for deaf people to furnish to those who serve them. $.60

Silent Siren
A fold-out wallet card with 57 signs useful to police and law officials, including suggestions for communicating with the deaf. $.25; 5/$1.00, 20/$3, 100/$10

Pre-pay all orders from individuals; add 10% of order for postage and handling, to $5 (actual shipping beyond that). Write for quantity prices, bookstore discounts, and other information.